READ EVERYTHING I WRITE, POOR SPELLING, GRAMMER AND ALL, WITH A FINE ENGLISH ACCENT. (OXFORD OR BETTER). IF BOOK IS COVERED IN PLASTIC, AND THIS IS ALL IMPORTANT, PLEASE REMOVE SLOWLY TO PREVENT BULLSHIT FROM FALLING OUT. TO ACHIEVE OPTIMUM RESULTS, READ WITH THE BLUES PLAYING SOFTLY IN THE BACKGROUND. FOR BETTER RESULTS, YOU MAY DECIDE TO SIMPLY PRETEND TO ENJOY THE STORY INSIDE REGARDLESS ON HOW BAD. FOR EVEN BETTER RESULTS, READ WHILE TOTALY STONED. TO INSURE QUALITY OF SUCH LITERATURE, I HAD SO HOPED FOR MARYJUANA TO BE, BY NOW, LEGALIZE THROUGHOUT THE ENTIRE WORLD FAR PRIOR TO THIS BOOK HITTING (US) SHELVES IN THE HOPES OF SELLING AT LEAST ONE COPY. PERHAPS IT WOULD END UP A BEST SELLERS LIST? OPEN TOE,,,,, IF YOU ARE IN ANY WAY AQUAINTED WITH A HYPNOTIST, IT MAY BE WISE TO INVITE HE OR SHE TO STAND CLOSE BY IN THE INSTANCE YOU FIND CONVINCING YOURSELF AS WELL AS OTHERS THAT THIS BOOK IS WELL WORTH YOUR HARD EARNED CASH A BIT DIFFICULT AND YOU REQUIRE A REFUND. BY THE WAY, I HAVE A GARAGE FULL OF THEM SO PLEASE, BY ALL MEANS, KEEP THE DAMN THING. RIGHT, WITH THAT BEING SAID, YOU ARE NOW READY TO BEGIN. CONFIDENTALY, NONE OF THE NAMES HAVE BEEN CHANGED TO PROTECT THE INNOCENT. THERE ARE NO INNOCENT. YOU MAY NOW OPEN THE BOOK..... ENJOY. OH YEA, DO NOT FORGET THE ACCENT.

TOINEN

TOINEN'S

Lövsångaré

All Correspondence, Book Orders and
Proceeds C.O. Amnie Stoakley (CEO)

Book p (US OFFICES)

P.O. box 402

Royal Oak, MI

48068 (USA)

MYEXTRAORDINARY9FEARSOFMONUME
NTS@ROCKETMAIL.COM

CLINCH YOUR BUTTOCKS; THE WORLD IS FAR WIDER THAN ANY HUMAN MIND MAY CONCIEVE. Never fear, I promise to keep it LINOTYPED.

Prepare Ur -self. My works read as instruction on life.

Die riesige weiße Giraffe (The Giant White Giraffe)

Das Ziehen (The Pulls)

Züge und Riesen (Trains and Giants)

Die Furcht Vor Denkmälern (Fear of Monuments)

Der Regenraum (Regenzimmer) (The Rain Room)

Der Milchmann (The Milkman)

Verfluchter Hellseher (Cursed Clairvoyant)

Kochbuch für den einsamen hearted (Cookbook for The Lonely Hearted)

Der große Widerspruch (The Great Contradictor)

Der braune Waliser (The Brown Welshman)

D'rqutoi Höschen (D'rqutoi Knickers)

Ihr blauer peocock (Her Bleu Peacock)

Der Liebling (THE FAVORITE)

Mitt Rum

Der Elch des Zeitreisens (The Elk of Time Travel)
You Are PLURAL

The Kidnapping of Jude Brown

Contradiction of a Pessimist

NU TXT MSG

Der Geschichtserzähler.

ELUDING KARMA

The Ditherer

If you have never formally, the pleasure, nor
privilege of reading my previous work, all
written in (9) languages. Word of mouth Press.
Mainly reserved for A Select Few. Never mind
GOOGLE, you may never find them. Simply
wait until you are asked.

This book has one Chapter. (CHAPTER): noun; A main division of a book. As described by every known source on the planet, considering the subject is Literature. This is One story, One subject, with One beginning and One Absolution. My Lazy O-Level insures the reader walks in my shoes. For instance, If I say, (Exposed duct work on a 20ft flat black painted ceiling cornering my left eye to catch a single fallen snowflake through the crystal clear window of a Greenwich Village Loft Conversion as my childhood and Mortality draws me to tears). You are there. You sit in that very room. You draw a tear, captured in thought of your own Mortality. "Why do you cry?',, asked a friend or near-by stranger. " It is this book", you answer. Your friend borrows the Book or better still, buys a copy. Opposed to, If I say, (Exposed duct work (,) on a 20ft flat black painted ceiling (,) cornering my left eye, etc., etc.,). It pauses the reader's brain. Releasing him back to his world, instead of where I need him to be.

In Mine.

TOINEN

(FICTION): Noun; Lit in the form of prose; as described by Oxford Dictionaries. Something told or written that is never fact, Merriam-Webster. But I were there, Remember. Fiction may take many forms. Fiction often tackles Truth, wrestles it to the ground. And after the bell has gone, struts proudly about the ring. Its right hand stretched upward. Golden chalice in hand, and a slight echo of a short lived, soon forgotten crowd of onlookers, whom have now left it standing in an empty arena, without an inkling of what has taken place before their very eyes. Fiction, Based on Total truths as dictated by Herself. Main Subject. (SHE). Now there's a word. I have had the pleasure of reacquainting myself on numerous occasion. One might go so far as to say, I have kept really good books. A Journal of sorts. Her every Word, Action, Movement, Thought. Her Pain. In fact, though unseen by all, excluding myself, of course. Found me aboard the very aircraft the day our esteemed Miss, granted herself, (Our Gift to the World). And in what I had so hoped would be our final meeting place, I find her once again. A Book? A Statement? A Confession? A Healing. Finding one's self. Acceptance. This Story finds itself, Loves itself, finds Love, then Breaks your Heart.

(Schizophrenia): Oxford Dictionaries describes it as, (A long- term Mental Disorder of a type involving a breakdown in the relation between thought, emotion and behavior leading to faulty perception) etc. But life has better prepared me for the perceptions of Man, and his many Definitions. Born from fear and a need to adumbrate facts, Which May Result in Worlds Wide Cataclysm.

A.H.S ffitch

THE AUTHOR-NARRATOR (Finnish Author, Toinen)

Genius? Scholar? Honorary Vicar, or Madman. A Mother. (2) Children, their births stem (9) years from one another. A Grandmother. Butcher, Baker, Candlestick Maker. A Seven in One Stroke. FINNISH. 9th born of (10) children. An English O level, often ignored. Born Thursday, November 27, 1969. A Thanksgiving Day to be exact. Aboard a family owned, Lier Jet. Somewhere between Trollhättan and Geneva. Speaker of (9) languages. Never speaking a word, nor setting foot upon (US) shores before the age of (9). Why may you never speak, asked her Mother on her 9th Birthday. Her answer? Human Beings are complete, utter Idiots. She were Immediately spanked and sent off. "I Professed to know very little, knowing nearly all before such an age", she now says, interrupting (us). Me, as always. Her accent, HIDDEN. "I wish to speak as an American", she says. With the year rounding to 1980 who would listen to a NOT to (8) year old, or any child. Gibberish, they would have said. Now off to your room. If I speak, you shall learn something from it or I keep well buttoned. Upon conversation with me, speak properly, be kind. Teach me something or you have lost me. My intention is to educate my reader, without taking him to school". Spending countless years between Geneva and Sveden. "Having been Born Sky, or there -in, One never really feels at home anywhere", she said. Now, as we except everywhere and London as home base. Have recently returned to the (US). The Midwest, of all places. In search of Hope, Sanctuary, Peace, and that Monet Original, hanging silently in the Detroit Institute of Arts, displaying her Favorite flower of the same name, Gladiolus. "That I shall one day Own", she said. An Extreme Clairvoyant. Greek Historian. Viticulturist. " I drink solely Left Bank", she now says, smiling stupidly, as she dangles an empty Red Wine goblet from her right pinky. A Paranoid. And one of the most wide opened relationship with the Dearly Departed than the Forbidden Book of a similar name. "My Parents are born (9) years from one another", she says. Daddy being the eldest. A constant struggle, my phobias. (40) or more. "They hinder me", she said. There being no proper care outside the walls of Switzerland, my struggle persists, as I travel this Globe. As I recall Scientist near the Swiss Alps ponder to explain how one living being could ultimately find any possible use for 90% of the brain's power, all of the conscience hours in one day. She is doing this with very little effort, I recall one of them to say. This is an acute Danger to her health, Extremely dangerous for the rest of us. Long live my slumber. PLUVIOPHILE: Lover of the Rain. My constant need to feel clean in a Filthy World. MEGALOPHOBIA: Megalo; Greek, translation, Large. A Fear of large things or My Fear of Power, Authority and so forth and so forth. Heal Thyself. While medical compensate their lifestyles, now medical may pay me. I no longer need the Doctors. I now know who I am. What I am. Why I am here. Why they have left me here. Why I never fit in. And why asking why may be yet another one of man's greatest Sin. (A.S)

ICEBREAKER

Rooting for The Good Thief. Peace of Mind. A
Fine English accent on Beautiful Brown skin. A
natural Blond behind the wheel of a Matte
Black on black C-Class. Brit-Coms. A Bottom
Crescent Moon. Unless I May purchase inner
piece, I need never, Money. Champagne and
Wedding cake. The Locksmith as the Thief.
Flower Lab Moscow. When I like something,
and wish to see more but there never is. The
involuntary fight to live: Meaning; THIS
SENTENCE HAS BEEN DELETED FOR MY
SAFETY AND YOURS. The Rain. Greek
Mythology. Black walls Chandeliers and
Wrought Iron. What is an Episode of
EastEnders minus Fat Boy??? I would never
intrude on your home, nor ascertain your
location there of as I proceed in the removal of
evil spirits. Nor shall it ever incur a fee. How I
had longed to die by Daddy's side in well
attired tear-filled conversation descending my
head to my lap as he asked more than twice
"What is the matter". And just as my head
collapse into his hands the last words I hear
were to be, (Oh AM). But I realize now that I
wish him never, hurt in wonder as I now have
in reality and confusion of his own Death.
Cognac colored Leather. President Jimmy

Carter. My 46th Birthday where I shall start the first day of my 47th year. How did I work that out you asked? Come now, none of we have been born a year old now have we? If so, Please, by all means, write me and we shall discuss it. AT LENGTH. Exposed Duct work on a 20ft flat black painted Ceiling cornering my left eye to catch a single fallen snowflake through that crystal- clear window of a Greenwich Village Loft Conversion as my childhood and Mortality draw me to tears. I have, at this very moment, splashed out £200 in less than (20) minutes on one pair of Black Skinny Boot cut Jeans inside a Mall on a Tuesday Morning before Noon. Just who the H@ll do I think I am? REPATITION. The Brown Welshman. Dear Fiber Optics, please re-attach the coiled cord to my phone so that I may never move four feet from the kitchen and may never read a screen which displays the words, NOT REGISTERED IN YOUR NETWORK. My Son. People need Heroes, I just need People. Foggy Rainy weather. When Cameron says "Ferris, you don't understand, he never drives it, he just rubs it with a diaper". We may eat an entire fortnight at £200. A constant flowing stream of headlights shining through that same snowfall past 6pm as I walk to my favorite Cigar House. Feeling the warmth of Blue string lights inside my room, so is the one I love, or at least I wish. The Lois Hill Granulated Collection. (11) minus (2) are (9). Vintage everything. A man with a tiny wallet and Great Style. Never that Life has yet to imitate Film. More to the point, Film has yet to imitate Real Life. Dear Super Sexy Smoking Hot Birmingham Stock Dude, Dark hair in the Red Trainers, where have you Gone? A good high, blue string lights and I am with You. Girls NEVER refuse your man (face) time. The proteins in Semen reduce fine lines and wrinkles (wink). ©2012. And now may we sit as this last statement is grabbed from our very fingertips whilst we wait patiently watching our favorite soap only to find ourselves interrupted by soft piano and a voice with a jar of face cream Now with A Remarkable New Ingredient by some strange Scientific name, we shall then proceed to google to ascertain meaning of the long word for SPERM. A silent Power as such may I never own, nor acknowledge. Power being that it is Man's Second Greatest Sin. As (the devil) or (a), may find unbearable, a Kilometer's walk in my shoes, the average, or so called average child may find they have little to no choice. Choose-eth not The Bestseller based on mere punctuation, spelling, dictation multiplied by (2) divided by Book sales alone. More so on the depth of the story the ingenuity the Balls of the storyteller. People Congregating to help. Notice, I did not say Strangers. We are NOT Strangers. Education and Intelligence are gifts, neither of which are obtainable through books nor Educational establishments. The Blues. A Dark Brown Leather Campomaggi bag. Or Wallet. A Heart Broken Violin. They Might Be Giants, best name for a Band, or anything. I have lived the whole of a year aboard a Phillip Starck without once having jumped into the Sea. (FEAR). A background of Bass Cello. Kent in Winter. Have you ever looked closely at an American $100 Dollar Bill?,,,, The look on Benjamin Franklin's face suggest, (NOW JUST WHAT HAVE YOU DONE TO AQUIRE ME AND AREN'T YOU ASSHAMED?) Describing myself as I am, never the person I (aught) be, never the person you assume I should have by now become. The Dark may never merely remain Dark due to ill light, night fall or lack of a good strong match. Dark are grouped living Entities. I recall one Summer's morn as we had been warned prior of temporary Black out. The Moment of Darkness awakened me singing softly, Harmoniously, (Arise, for we are here). Chico De Barge is gone really give me what I want. Anything Philip Starck. Hope never, in the miss-spell-meant of his name. World Travel between March and May, but never at the weekend. Have you noticed that I have never capitalized (the or devil)? Black and White music video in full slow-mo with absolutely nothing to do with the songs meaning or lyrics and no one is singing. The Welsh. Fresh Ice-cold Root Beer. Toinen's Father. Folded crisps. Liking neither the game nor the player. Repetition is king. Or is it,, Masturbation is King,,, I forget. Classic Film starring Joan Blondell. Recalling my Copyright to add this very quote: (My main Beast of Burden, confined in the walls of this book which I have so painstakingly, wrist twistingly torn upon you. I now realize that I really give far less than a damn. At this very moment realize that I never actually have, and at my age, no longer (haf) nor care to. Nor should one ever condemn another based upon any form of past behavior or treatment towards another for they have long come from remaining the same person from one year to another. But I refuse to rewrite this whole thing so PLEASE, try and enjoy). Celebrating May 6th, 1977 when I am

(7) years old, discovered that I am never wet when under water, but only after passing through the surface. ©1977. Since I have presented this rough draft, i.e. the first (3) supposedly chapters, manuscript to numerous Literary agents, I assume like everything else, my discovery has been stolen by now. But never fear for I have yet to be brainwashed to the belief of someone else discovering it. ©1977. NEVER EVER THINK OF STEALING IT. The 2011 Saab (95), Scion Auto motives' Crowning Glory. Retro Cartoons minus an alphabet. Flip what back to front???? European Travel in the Autumn. A king- sized Dove White Comforter on the reduced wrack of an Anthropologies shop on a Sunday before noon. Today as I return from the Post there were (9) minutes left on the meter. The Sleepy Jackson. Small rooms with Large furniture. Cognac Leather seats in an all-Black Mini interior. Circumnavigation. Circumcision. When someone really attractive has access to an extremely powerful telescope and a clear view of my bedroom window. So name one thing wrong with making a complete fool of yourself. The Elk of Time Travel. An American Standard FENDER Stratocaster with a Rosewood Fretboard Solid Teak Body and

Pearl Pickguard. Shabby Chic Décor done in all Black. A huge Sephora VIB Rouge Haul. LONDON at Sundown. A Louie XV Canapé dimly lit by a Tiffany Original floor lamp in the front Drawing room of a Charcoal Grey painted Brick Queen Anne backing a South Facing Garden of an overgrown un- manicured Wild Flower laced lawn seen from across a Cobblestoned Dual Carriageway. Smoke is neither Sin nor Triumph, but a mere addiction. When a single raindrop hits the crown of a Black rubber Wellie. West Canfield Street in Mid-town Detroit. Love. A rainy weathered walk in a knee length floral Silk Chiffon dress bare foot inside Black Steel Toe Harness ankle boots and no umbrella. (41) and (14) are (55). Oatmeal colored Wool in Winter. A fresh bolt of crisp White Linen at £22 a yard. My Granddaughter, and the fact that I am only (44) years old. AWESOME. Tiny white string lights on a dark background, or anywhere. GOD. The Brown Welshman. Repeating myself. Classic Mini. Sense, or Since wearing TOM FORD'S Tobacco Vanille Fragrance, I find that I am smoking far less than before. Oh no, I never pose, I said, if you catch me in sexy mode for heaven's sake Capture the Foto, this is a rare occasion. (YES, FOTO). Condensating Rain drops on the warm Chrome Metal bumper of that 1963 Split Window Mitchell Stingray parked solely outside a Neon Lit Mum and Pop Camper Conversion Diner on a (60) Degree rainy Wednesday night. John Cooper Works. My Daughter's Voice. A 2am PRAYER. Harry and Draco standing side by side. A Davidoff (3000) lit by a Sulfate free match and a stranger's hand. The fact that at 7:45 pm on May 6th, 2007 I had a thought, why never apply Braille to Currency so that our Visually Impaired are never short changed, and If someone profits from this idea and I am never crowned Thrillion-aire by Opening Bell?,, so be it. While we stand here, why not treat balding the way we treat bare spots in our lawns. Sod? A rug which grows to the scalp. Sounds a bit dangerous. An extra 40% off after final sale price. My Daughter's Laughter. The smoke and indifference found in a small fume filled café off the beaten track of Montmartre as we disagree on the smoking ban in pubs. My Daughter's Smile. Would I were a man, I would be Jackie Coogan as the kid in the 1921 film of the same name starring Himself alongside Charlie Chaplin. Babies drinking from a sippy cup. My Son's voice. Building a bridge to connect towns and people, then the realization of maintenance costs after (2) years, and I have burned the bulk of the profit on shoes. The hopes that maybe one day I may never wake from that perfect dream of Love where I wish to remain being as I am far too old to deal with reality. And before I can take it all in, my Mobile rings and here I am, Back to Shit. The lights of Times Square seen from an anger filled native of NY Cabby driven taxi. Things of which others have little or no knowledge, Like Amnieotonics. ©2009 Unpublished Theory; (AMNIEOTONICS): ©2009. The Little-known fact that this lovely Planet we call home has many dark secrets, One being her daily shift. For instance, on most days I find more than enough room to past between Bed and Armoire, other days I may barely squeeze by without ever shifting my furniture, although my Son says "Mom, it's already a thing". White smoke. The smell of burning wood crackling. Snowfall. Beauty. A well Auctioned Claude Monet Original. Never growing up because I were never a child. Never growing old because I am born an old woman. Men who still love Ming. The common misconception of Dracula, being that She is a He. Had She been a He, surely his name would be pronounced and spelled Dracul. You know, minus the (A). Being of male origin, blah blah, blah, U get it! Considering, of course, the country of origin. Who is to say Dracula, or Dracul, is bred from any one corner of the Globe. Taupe colored anything. Wondering how, from the time I entered 2nd grade till now, the word (Color) has developed a (u), now it is spelled (Colour). Must be Global Warming. Keeping sure my legs are always 1/2 shade darker than my shoes, rendering me virtually naked. Scoring that perfect bottle of South Eastern Australian Petite Syrah for under £10. The fact that my Son has the ability to and will explain the meaning and purpose of anything, In Detail. When my Children use the phrase (Thanks Mom), it puts a diaper on my ever- reoccurring shitty days. The Live Blues I hear outside an old squeaky paint chipped rust hinged woodworm and termite devoured once screened door swinging in a warm summer night's breeze holding an ice-cold Miller high life in hand that makes me wish you were mine, or at least somewhere nearby. Just one day ago I stood for half an hour next to a sign stating NO STANDING. I have decided to stay indoors today, just in case they're looking for me. WATER. A Black on Black FIAT Abarth with Chinese Red Calipers and red and black Leather seats. Repeating myself. Safe, Happy, Healthy Children and Grandchildren. That same inexpensive bottle of Syrah chasing a perfectly spoon twirled fork of mushroom shrimp spinach coated Fettuccini. Fresh, Clean, Crisp, Wintery Morning Air. Or my day ending eye locked on an Oversized Local Artist rendition of Grand Master Flash on a freshly sandblasted brick wall as I hear the third or fourth repetition of the chorus during an Amateur Rap Battle in Mid-Town Detroit. A 1971 Jaguar without a scratch in its original Pistachio Factory color spotted quicker than not through the clear glass floor to ceiling freshly sponged plate glass window while speeding past a shotgun showroom tucked snugly under a huge slowly spinning sign which simply reads "USED CARS". This Book could use more Cow Bell. That old familiar smell of a burning Marlborough Red (100) soft pack. Or the passing whiff of one who has smoked them man and boy. The critics whom shall deplore such attitude. My unpaid attentions on when to use, WHO and WHOM, and SENSE and SINCE. My constant confusion about when to use Who and Whom. A point (.925) copper based Sterling Silver Skull ring on each finger of my right hand purchased from Dead Ringers. I definitely shan't be capitalizing the word critics. And though you may very well capture Ghostly images on film, maybe never expect them to hang around long enough to show anyone else. A dream I have yet to fulfill. Live horns. Contradictions. Empire of The Sun's Music causing me to love and want to be Loved. An oversized Union Jack blowing in a Westerly London breeze. Laughing at the fact that I have lived all these years just to arrive at Sorrow and Nothingness. A fresh bolt of White eyelet. Navy taupe and charcoal with a hint of green. Dried Dead Roses. Halloween. The Autumn. I were once Loved by a Beautiful Man. A Montana (US) Sky. Why not have we Edited the Story. "It's sure to be a Best Seller", they said. Do you never wish to profit (1) Million Euros? I May. But then there shall I remain. Stuck, stood standing in the Hereafter, trying my DAMDEST to explain why the FUCK I felt as though I require the whole of a Million Dollars in one, single Lifetime parallel to those who survive the day in lack of (3) square meals. (Greed-Sin). A Black salt stained Mercedes C- 550 dirty from the slushy conditions of a Midwest winter parked wheels faced outward the curb sandwiched between some puke colored Pinto and an old Ford Pick-up. Watching Classic Scooby Doo Movies on a rainy Saturday morning while sipping Best Quality Cheyenne Pepper Corn laced Hot Cocoa topped with Fresh Creamy Real Whipped Cream from a heavy duty chipped white China tea cup and no saucer. 1940's Topper Returns starring H.B Warner, Billy Burk And Eddie Rochester. Merely We Live, starring Billy Burke and Constance Bennett. Heated coil tires which melt black ice on contact. © 2016. A Snow White Classic Porsche constructed from a solid sheet of steel with Midnight Blue Leather interior. Is it the lovely clicking sound you get from setting an All Clad LTD to the Hollow Molecules of a custom built Charcoal Black Soapstone Apron Sink? Or the knowledge of living in a world where Iceland is Green and Greenland is Cold as a H@ll? The Evil shyness of a Full Moon peaking from dark clouds. The final scene in The Breakfast club when Molly Ringwald places a single diamond stud in the palm of Judd Nelson's hand. The words (Audio slave). Film starring Edward Furlong. The fact that we all go to a h@ll, for a while anyway. Apparent Ghost. The Planet Jupiter. Being Sagittarius. Any Auto-mobile manufactured prior to the 1980's. Porcelain

Busts. An 18th Century natural colored Limestone Mantel against a smoke grey or black wall. The dimly lit ambiance of Restoration Hardware shops. Claude Monet's rendition of my most favored Flower, Gladioli, currently on display at The Detroit Institute of Arts which I plan to nick but lack the cherries. Classic Lupin the third (III) Cartoons. Being (44) years old and learning only yesterday that the word (slowly) has no E. Thank Heaven for spell check. Being (44), I love double digits. Mergers, i.e. Yamamoto Adidas, Benz Honda, Peugeot Citroen, Porsche Audi, Chocolate and Peanut butter, Ralston Purina, Anheuser Busch, Moet Hennessey, Pot Holes and the Wheel Alignment profession, MINI AND COOPER, etc. Now if we could just convince NASA and Depends to shake hands on millions and millions of little teeny tiny undergarments. Then we could bring DHL, UPS, and FED-EX on board to distribute them to all of the birds all over the World. The fact Beauty and the Beast are one in the same. The fact that I shall never feel freedom to move and shake on a dance floor, or share true love and friendship. Unfinished Wedgewood floors at the Foot of a freshly paint stripped white washed from blue based banister-ed staircase.

The fact that I shall never be liked just for being me. (Better yet, scratch that,,,,,,, Found Someone). OR SO I HAD THAUGHT. Matte Black on Matte Black backing. Calamari. Tomatoes are my favorite fruit. Extra Hot Chicken Shrimp Pad Thai with a side plate of Freshly vine ripened red tomatoes and a tall glass of pineapple juice with a splash of Rum. Any Danny Elfman Composition. Squinting my right eye to catch that unknown glimpse of Horse and Carriage stained on the memory of time outside a Centuries Old Manor House. Never morning for her but for the women she were either robbed of being or never allowed to become. Sleeping like a full fresh nappy'd infant soon after a Warm milk feeding. Black Bamboo floors. All my things fitted neatly into a 21" 100% Authentic Black Horn Back Crocodile double handled Hobo bag standing Red-eye Northbound the tarmac, my Son by my side ready to board a small Boeing headed Duty bound Zealand on a surprise visit where we shall hug my Daughter and Grandchild for about an hour or until I am asked to let go. Sushi. A Diamond Left Pinkie Ring on the Arrogant Bastard who has just hurt my feelings. This unfortunate, overwhelming sometimes remarkable habit of remembering every second, of every hour of every day of my torrid little life. Dark Navy eye-shadow on Olive skin. Never opening my mouth unless you may learn something from it. A (16) Hand Irish Born Arabian Stallion. A Tim Burton Film. The Granger, Harmon, Lucas combination on an episode of Are You Being Served. Today I witnessed (4) low-Flying planes. My unheard laughter as I Stand unseen, at the look upon your face as you read my tombstone stating nothing more than, "(Anything To Get Out Of MICHIGAN)". Had I known who or what I were, at the very least I could own up to it and stand proud. Saving everything to Cassette and VHS. No matter what technology brings, nothing may outlive the common motor. Even if I have to crank it by hand. Telling my Children and Grandchildren that if I am not buried in Milton Keynes, I shall wait well after they have removed their Funeral attire and fallen fast asleep following the drunken laughter filled party held in celebration of my passing. I shall knock at the door, and standing there in full Dead state, my eyes blaze red, as mother once described doing, were we to ever leave a dirty dish in any sink. Even our own sinks, in our own homes. I am stood there chuckling from the looks on their faces as I insist they have me exhumed and flown home at the double. My undying fear of monuments or anything towering more than (2) feet above my head. The overwhelming, chest arresting angst, Beautiful, Humbling feeling of a plain eyes view of someone who has taken (20) times the effort, as I assumed my appearance to be flawless a mere (2) seconds before laying eyes upon them as they walk past in full self-awareness unaware of my best efforts brand new outfit and hairstyle. Prayer. I have embarked on many a journey. Each holding a more fascinating name and meaning as the one prior. LIFE, having been one of the Longest, Most Tedious. Certainly the only physical one. (WANT), The healthiest of Sin. Having one of the longest email addresses in the World, (myextraordinary9fearsofmonuments@rocketmail.com). Thank Heaven for Autofill. 2am Prayer. The long anticipation of my Death as I lay facing East,, This Time. What could be more beautiful than ice falling from the sky. Sitting here with little more to do than write this. Living the whole of my time just to arrive at PRAYER coupled with complete Happiness. The fact that you may Never, Ever, in your days, read a BOOK such as this. Perhaps you

shall read a better one. BUT NEVER
SIMULAR. (And my Strengths?): LIFE in itself;
Blink, and you may well have missed it.

A.S

At A Great War We
Invade One Another.

A.S

Toinen's

Lövsångaʁé

And Odyssey, (GREEK: Odysseia), ODYSSEUS. One of two Major, Ancient, Epic Greek Poems. Odyssey, A long adventure filled voyage, from Poetry of Ancient Greece. Homer's Epic Hero, Odysseus, fought bravely on distant shores before embarking on the journey to his native land. Much like the Character in this story, Odysseus too lost his way and wandered, yet remaining resolute ultimately finding his way. Proper Remuneration, (REMUNERATION): or Payment. Compensation. A phrase which often comes to mind upon a long gaze of her face. And When, may I ask, shall she receive? Between each tear which follows. As our beloved character, this story too is a Disambiguation. (DISAMBIGUATION): Word Sense; To establish a single grammatical or semantic interpretation for. Quite the odd misfortune I have to recall each hour of each day of her torrid life. Played out like an overrated Broadway com-eth. Eluding all critics. Placing itself in the top (10), for yet another Decade." I may never recall if I am living, alive, or merely given a similarity of days following my Death", she says. A play as you will. A continuation of what may have happened, had my life gone further. I am buried somewhere. Might it be England? A Grand Tombstone with my name boldly engraved. Do my children weep? Does my Grandchild understand? "I am but a tortured soul. Lowlight to dark. Fear to hurt. Pain. More pain. Now run, hide. Want, need, burn. Cry loudly while you are there hiding, Mother would say. "The time now reads 4pm and I fancy my demise on a rainy day", she said. It is cold when the chill strikes only me. Declared motionless. Alone, in a world of many. While others laugh, play, sure of their fate. Themselves. But oh, what Fiendish thoughts, this one. Why must I face this alone, I had often wondered. Not much looking forward to now, sept my dinner. Then so to bed, for a fresh take on yet another Butts path for school joking's. And guess who blocks thy path? Most intolerable, my time on a dark course where she now lives, in fear. Never her own, but others. And though totally inconsolable, wares the same ridiculous, hurt hidden smile to this very day. Yes, it is dark where she lives, very dark indeed. The trouble maker among us. Lonesome in a house of Billions. Few such as herself. Gifted really, in a world of so few. "O how must thy cope"? I ask. But our fair lady kept well buttoned for fear of releasing means by powerful passion. What she ponder, shall remain unseen. Few pages tell but a mere tale of what has taken we. Yes we, a lifetime to concede. Past tense?, A fallacy. We never really grow up. We merely learn to control the child within. ©2012. An ever so ailing, feverish, deteriorating mind. Her sickening childhood. Her parents. The Rich, The Poor. The constant need to feel clean in this filthy world. (Molysmophobia): The fear of Dirt, Infection. The hunger to nourish. "It has all been a lie", she said. Or were I ever meant to fit in a world which treated me special. Even more special than the perfect, or so called. No wonder the Dead, or who we perceive as Dead, always seem to flock at my door. Never entering, as I had inadvertently shed menstrual blood at my threshold. Keeping the strange and frightening at bay, as arms and vices reach for me at every turn. "No", she said. I have never fit here. "You shall never be the adult your age suggest", she now says to me. You drain and devour as does the Eucalyptus. Soaking up it's (300) liters of water for the day. "Consume?", I asked screaming. "Consume"? How dare you", I cry. My voice cracked in fear. Consumption as I stand here?, I ask. Consumption at my window day long, watching others consume. Watch as they leave, office attired, behind the wheels of auto loans as hours pass. Now return to Bank owned flats, automatic car park doors open, then close. And in Piss - Zip return time, they emerge, smiling in a slow trot. Dog leeded, yes LEEDED. Any excuse to drain workplace alcohol, only making room for night time drunkenness. Now tuck the hounds and thine offspring to bed with after (6) stilettos to fall madly into another with one whom we have never before met. Then rise early, do it once more in a thunderbolt of again, in order to provide. "If I stamp the ground, causing a large hole beneath. Would you fall to a h@ll, where you belong? Or simply hover above in that haze of Bullshit", she says, as she interrupts my lone concentration with a sinister tone. Call me Ishmael, for I am no man's underling. (UNDERLING): Noun; Derogatory;. One lower in status or rank. I recall one trip to the shops. No, never on Halloween. Never Thee, one day when the Dead walk undisclosed among us. Or have never, you once noticed", she said. It is (30) degrees colder than need be as the gates are open. Coldest day of the year. As we approached a man walking with his (2) sons. "Oh", I say smiling gracefully. How lovely they are. Then, in one instance, all changed. They see me before I see them. Their smiles and eyes drop. Heads turn to Father in disbelief, as he reassures them, ' Yes, he says. She does see you''. See, I told you, he said, as their heads turn in wait my eye catch-eth. Locked In Fear. Their feet freeze on common ground. Now reassure them twice leading them past, as the gaze, stare, drop me (3) below my heart. Confused I stand, as my Son has now led me too, away. "No Mom", he said. They are Monsters. And while far too lovely to be anything just, I concur, remember, dissect what I have seen. Recall the faces of mere children, who have now changed at the site, YES, site of me. "Yes, she can see you", his response. The Father of all Fathers, Minus my own, in regards to my stare. What could they possibly have been? Ghost. Demons more like. Demons. Of The Highest ,,,,,, (GH) again. English, what a language. The disbelief of me or my ability to spot an otherwise tortured soul, not only stunned, angered, amazed. Upset them. Sending forth a feeling of ill repute as I stumble to caress my own lost soul in a public place laced for the normal. Never one special, such as myself. How had my Son known, yet given less than a Damn as he walk- on as if little is shocking. Angered at what I may ill afford. Those left to hold. Those in which for I may never return? Trade thy gift for Riches? Never. O such aggravating, nagging senses reel me, ruining an otherwise dismal encounter with the shops. But once again I retire defeated. Lost. Who the Bloody Heck am I, and why? Who the Blooming Blazes are we? Me, my offspring.? What the H@%ll am I, and when? Alone. Solitaire, though my offspring harbor like. No obsession, as I pray screaming. No one lay eye upon me or perhaps they keep wwatchful that eye. Watchful with 2 small double v's. For I claim no such perfect and may lack luster ability to gaze upon those who are watching. Among my many gifts or curses, Time Travel. Unlike she who desires a Time machine. A most heinous, ugly craft. Almost a decade and 1/2 now, my most favorite Actor has passed. I, in most heartbreak fling my ignorant soul and mind a 1/2 decade prior that sad event. All is well now, I ponder. We are together and he knows me. A most wondrous journey, I thought as we are best of friends loving as we (laff). And as our encounter draw to a cheery close, he caresses my arm and with loving eyes looking deep to mine his soul speaks minus one less ounce of loving care, and I QUOTE,, I Love You, I care for not only you but for your very salvation. A very dangerous quest is to venture past ones' rest. END QUOTE. Our embrace and separation residue no hostility or barking but pure Love. I have never sense or since, for heaven's sake to venture past my own conscience, asleep or awake. A craft of the Sick and Never for me. Once used on past and present bullies, as I send their dreams to a h@ll observing as they scream, flee from uncommon fears. I chuckle till a following school day. One of them with the balls of satan actually with all remorse asked me to please leave them alone. How embarrassed I felt as they descend from that time to show me the utmost respect. Scary. Entering ones dreams, pure evil and none less than. (Sin). The bully is a devil as one more brutal than the rest has met me with the eyes of H@te. Demanding I educate him in thy very art. Evil Envy, (Sin). We all envy with little knowledge. It is lack of knowledge, forces envy. "You have all been fooled", she shouts, interrupting me yet again. The real Sins...Fear, Power, Self-Deprecation, Untruth from thy foolish lips, Exaggeration, Dissatisfaction, In contentment. Want and or an inability to seek freedom from. Repeating the words, (and or).

The contradiction of others to their faces. Negative response. Foul language, in any language. Refusal of assistance. Overuse of Automobile emissions (i.e.) Driving at more than high speeds. Animal Harnessing. Anger. Tattoos (Though I harbor several). The inhalation of fume (Tho, yes THO, I covet Davidoff 3000). Opinions. Envy. Though ever so stylish, The use of an umbrella. To administer punishment. Doubt. Disbelief. The criticism of ones Writing. Editing ones Writing. (Never Sure If Despising The Seemingly Happy is a bad thing, but I will SURELY Get Back To You On That). I somehow suspected this story to end far before I had found my way. After all, there is only so much technology, so much paper, so much printer ink, and so few years in one's life. Then, one day, as I awakened, I remembered. Who I had been, or were. Why I am here. My arrival. Occasions on which I could have returned and refused. How hard this journey would be, and why. It has now become clear. Where I am from, and how I have come to pass. Is the World, this World, the one chosen for me, any easier than one chosen for others?. It is all a test, a game? An assignment or quest. I am the Alien among us,, or one of. It saddens me now, never locating the others. Spending the entire time in solitude. Never knowing what to look for, or who. Nor what to look for in them. Were they, the so- called stars? The Extraordinary I have mentioned prior to? The Inventers, The Holey men? Opportune times to leave when ready, though suicide forfeits lost, starting another journey new, or all over again. "I certainly did not want that", she said. Why I never fit. Never played life a true hand at his game. Never growing older. Never one day's labor for gain financial. No friends, because there is no one like me. Never here anyway. So called Friends, Friends? , That worrying itch like feather stems poking, nudging my shoulder in need of wiping free. I have always appeared taller, larger. Wise for my demographic. When I would speak the world paused. Moving slowly, yet further away. Why I always refer to everyone as Humans, or them. But you are not like them. Mother has always said. Had she known? So why all the while lay dormant, you ask. Quietly, unseen, watching. Waiting for a moment. A time which may never come. Still I wait. Seeing what others may never. Hearing what all may never. Remembering everything, Yes EVERYTHING. Every nappy change, even the ones which brought about pain. "I loved you dearly before remembering" she said, sadly. Clairvoyance is a powerful thing when used wisely. For (46) years I have taken in a planet and its inhabitants. A World built solely for me. Everything I heard, saw, felt, tasted, Feared, wondered about. Nothing,, Nothing more than a test. Un-real. It is the reason you celebrate Birthdays. "You ALL crave your Deaths", she shouted. But no one heard. Everything given life, Plants, Animals. The innocent Babies. My Dear, sweet Grandchildren. The nicest of the nice. The meanest of the mean. The baby lamb who ate so gently from my hand as so never to nip me. The most obedient of Equine. The believer, trying his damnedest to believe. All sent here for one purpose. To right a wrong. Make up for loss or lost time so to speak. This is H@*ll. Only in a h@ll would I trap my left pinky in an automatic revolving door crushing endlessly the nail plate piercing to mess its own bed. A mere set-up for a week of pain, as it heals slowly releasing the knife from raw meat to assume its rightful position. Only here will you see that perfect one you may never touch. Only here must one work to eat. The second most important necessity in sustaining life. In all we who have come, harbor a dark past. Remembered or forgotten, we must face this past. Our process to handling it results our fate. Yes, free will is too an Illusion. How may I seek higher than the (One GOD). Who my wishes he make-eth, YES, MAKE-ETH me dream hopeless. Yet for only what he hath in store. ©2015. "You are awfully quiet today", she said. "Yea, well", I said. Today I feel quite never as yet the pretender. Pass Off to the left hand. Death some say. A new beginning, as told by others. We, the Clairvoyant. From our highest of horses during the rainy season? Or are we merely pleased with ourselves like a good hair day. Or is our greatest Sin to leave the un-knowers unknowing? What we witness, shall we tell? "Me", she said, trembling. I have always been aware, watching. The lone witness. Answering, when answers were most unwelcomed. "I am merely lending a hand", she sprout shit forth exploding in time to be heard. For she is sent off, yet again. Far too late, this time, I am afraid. I dodge blood from thine own septum. Disbelieving is the disbeliever. Now weakened in state, why must thy hit. Now turn, walk quickly away, accompanied by throbbing fist and the haunting memory of the Angel you have struck. I suck my teeth three times. "Naughty

Human", I say, quietly shaking my head. "May I never speak my mind nor practice what I preach", she has said to me, on more than one occasion I can assure you. It ruins the face. Apart from which, no one really appreciates it anyway as my dear sister would later explain. We crave Leverage, a tinniest of power. Sin, non-less. And may I never possess the cherries to put my enemies in their places. It annoys the close minded and the clumsy. The whole conversation placed at an hour past (44), and about damn time in my books. Backing a comment shat out by Mother. Still breathing, affront long awaited comebacks. "And may he bless me never, with Whitty comebacks", she yelled. For Power is the monster we seek. ©2015. A brave girl this one. What a brave girl indeed. OSTENDERE:(LATIN), Verb. A Present Active Infinitive of (OSTENDO). "Meaning to Expose or Exhibit", she spits, interrupting me. "In similar acts witnesses out of the blue. Screaming the fact that Bill Gates is The Original Harry Potter, only after an ill attempt to pursued strangers and passers-by to believe Ichabod Crane must have been the reincarnation of The Headless Horsemen. Owing to the fact no harm had ever really come to him, when others seem to, as she put it, Lose Their Heads. The Madeline story, The life story of Oleg Cassini, shoe designer. What???? I recall on one occasion where she proceeded to explain to a couple how healthy the gentleman must have been owing to the very fact that the man has stumbled on pavement in plain view, the love of his life. "Proves to the world that you possess a good heart", she taunts in full vocal. "You Sir, have little to no evils", she says. Explaining in full detail how a devil may never slip. "He is sure footed", she says as the couple walks on in embarrassment. "Holds his head high", she shouts after the poor couple. "A wise man is humble as he proceeds face down watching his step for he may fall". To curse the devil is to wish slide catching himself in embarrassment through that puddle of spit-up, she continued on as the couple had hastily disappeared indoors. (These facts too, shall be stolen from my very grasp. As I have presented, (sed) literature, to more than half a dozen publishing houses). Never to mention, the help received (@) The Ferndale Public Library. (9) Mile road, Detroit. In the Midwest part of (USA). A promise to delete all visitors drafts upon closing of the doors. Deleted from our memory stick, is what I have been told, but I have my doubts. "But never fret", she contest with fist raised high, smiling and eager. "I shan't let you down", she now raves. Truth is truth. And the thief may never steal what were never rightfully his own". ©2009. The return of Disco, in Music anyway", she whispers, leaning towards me, tearing up for an acclamation. The end of Public Places, is one I can believe. With all this technology, who needs shops? Click a button, retrieve it from your doorstep. "Everything shall go online and underground", she raved. (ACCLAMATION): To Cry. Our second most common act. First, from where I am standing. The surface of the Earth shall grow Silent and still. Though I am never sure about vegetation. "Grow ramped", she said. Owing to the vast Automotive sales, we, or you Humans are slowly losing use of your legs." Unless of course you were blessed, born a New Yorker", I said Leaning ever so slightly to the right of (45), though childlike in nature. I am rolling today, or today seems much simpler, and less tedious on the wrist. It flows from me. This hurt, this angst. This need to free thy soul. Taking with it, the offspring, set forth from thy very womb, in the hopes that they too, may seek a freedoms path. "One day I shall be free", she said, I know I am at my

Crown. The flies are all about me at present.
They smell evil. No, never evil which stems
from said practice of. Evil. The same Evil
developed from a non-righteousness, coupled
with the impatiens and impurities of wonder.
"When"?, she asked. " Soon", I answered, in my
own impatience. I seek help, I have requested.
No reply. The doctors lowered their eyes and
changed the subject most visits. Your medical
may ill afford such help, I am told, when
seeking therapy in the States. Only for the
visit?,,, The non-help, the changing of the
subject, the pills to keep me asleep all day?...
To send you back home via Metro, till next
month and for his or her home, transport and
fancy clothes. Family will neither help nor
cognize. (COGNIZE): To Understand. Or at
least strive and. How could I live, when
everything made me ill? I could neither eat nor
bathe, fearing the touch of everything. (40) plus
phobias, all researched,, by me, myself. As I
struggle for a normal life. All my old
acquaintances are married, living their own
lives. I may never burden them. To aware my
Children may inhibit, as I have been dealing
with my own Mothers illness. "You need to
take care of me." My sister has been reformed
from an early child hood, by Mother. As a

result, she has never married nor bore Children of her own. No man, no home. Just a room where no friends embark. Happy to see my children moving forward, so I pretend to be, just ok. Still, they can see that ok is not. Had it been so, I would be fully employed. With a home and a life. The occasional ringing of my mobile. Never merely from them. They are in no way, Slow, as one may put it. They, in full aware of my, (Something may well be amiss with Momma -ness). But I smiled strongly as if this were premeditated. Oh no, I'm thru with men, I tell them. (Thruuu), Finite. All the while, longing for human touch. Never for the heartache which follows each relationship with a man. Even when I thought I had found the perfect one, Denmark went sour, once he realized I had no intention of paying him for his services. I have never, the need to pay a man to love me. This remains true. I am, have always been, and remain to this day, my own Damn Fool, no one else's. © 2016. Only when he learned the real me, did love fade. I shall never re- embark. No matter the number of Friday nights sat alone in a dark cell. I need never one more person from this Earth to know the real me. Soon the whole planet shall turn a shoulder at my arrival. Stare aimlessly at my departure. Till then I wish to quit whilst I am ahead. "Or have a head start", she said. I shall remain forever alone, delighted as such. Apart from the fact, I have left it a bit late to bother. Coupled with this blessing or curse, the knowledge of what each being within a (4) foot radius of me is thinking, ruins the fun. No one person is true. No one person cares for another. And no one person tells the truth. "They are all sad", she said. Hiding behind smiles of abuse and self-loathing. The World is a sham, and as I grew smarter, seemed less amused by my human shell and its function. No longer did I need transport, as I may think it and I arrive. I have lost the taste for food, the need for sleep. It is all wasted space, this life. A means for the Rich becoming Richer, while the un-educated and the un- interested stand on line for food and alcohol. "I am so alone, and sad", she said. I remember this the most. There are others close by and to them I wish to speak of my departure, though it too shall be down played to jokes and talks of things I care littler than shit about. Yes, LITTLER. (Get a Life). I play along well. As I grew weary of conversing with those who I care to never more set eyes upon after (46) years. "I wish never to think", she said. I like never, my thoughts. They are all bad. All past. All that is left are remembrances. Nothing to look forward to, so I keep looking back. No new memories or occurrences. All I do is to sit here, so how may I incur a new thought, encounter, or happening. The reoccurring thoughts of those who hurt me as a child in belief of my forgetfulness. In (2) cuffed hands, I hold harsh words, neatly tucked, secured, in fullest form. Capitalized and Highlighted. Festering under my right arm, stretched to strangle those, while never moving. Leaping close eye contact, as their necks crack under the pressure of my unseen tentacle. The disquietude attacks suffered from my age of (6). A result of inhabiting a home sub- inhabited by spirits of the lost. They take a great toll on the life of the young. Rendering me unable to function as normal, if there is such a meaning. I saw them when no one else would, so they took advantage. Leaning on me for solace. I found myself often sent off to Mitt Rum for talking to, well, what appeared to be myself. Mitt Rum. (My Room). The place I Dred, and the first place they looked for me. Most speaking the language of the cursed, which freighted me to an un-tear able state... Terrible, terrible. Before I learned to translate such terms. Things I may never share for fear of an unseemly destruction. Ripping body from soul. Terms one may never share for fear of my own safety and those of whom I still care for. They still, to this very day, play hide and seek. Finding me, though hundreds of thousands of miles away. I sit weeping. Still they find me. Hands on their hearts, however scary,,, they find me, begging for a release, or something. And my dreams of Napoleon, as he insist we are 80th cousins, or whatever. He pronounces, his right hand clutching for relief, the pain of Stomach Cancer. But there had been no known cure, not even as we speak. The ones known remain well guarded. Never so short, as I stand 170.18cm, when allowed to stand. We look eye to eye, in a grand indoors courtyard.. All his kings Horsemen in attendance. "These horses will filthy the floors"., I say to him to no avail. He just keeps well on. A well rounded speech. Preaching. Revealing to me his real intensions. How he is one of History's most misunderstood. How his names are slandered from truths. Why, he has been buried, cased in pure lead. The complete explanation of a deconstructed Pyramid. I listen, without Fear.. '.NO FEAR.'. And an unacquainted feeling of safety. I seek Capital, since or sense or since we are so related," I say.

(ENTITLEMENT): SIN. Or similar phrase from these stick vine lips, a similar statement has sent a far, well passed John Inman, fleeing from my grasp as fast and politely as you please. Money is to be shunned, I have heard on more than one occasion. Believe it or not, It has the ability to shorten one's life. Weaken ones path. I am hungry and in need of clean shelter. "Shun the currency" he states. No matter the origin. " Apart from which", he says, looking me in the eye as he grasp my right forearm, "No one need know of our meetings nor acquaintance". No one need know of our relation. Be warned my girl,, you do Not fancy THAT sort of Capital. There is such thing as too much, you see. I usually awaken before divulging my un-wish for Billions. Just a take-away, an apartment and a MINI Cooper, I wish to assure him. Oh, yea, and one of those Stainless Steel Fridges with big freezer drawer on the bottom. Perhaps an LG, the one with the LED lights. Maybe a Black, round, free standing, Soap Stone tub in a Bathroom with no commode. I want to get clean without puking my guts. (Fear of Drains): A condition so rare it has yet to be named.???? So I shall name it. How's about, Iwishnottolooktowardsthepitofhellmuchlessba

ckmyasssuptosituponitphobic. (or) Phobia.
Being in a white bath may assume I am in such
commode. YUK. Let's see, Black Bamboo
Floors. Or maybe unfinished, reclaimed,
Hardwood. With the large slats. A treadmill,
for my ever expanding ass. The (Stainless Steel)
Samsung, Wash/Dry front loaders are the best.
A Stainless steel Viking Stove, the industrial
type for Chefs, an open floor plan, two of
everything Restoration Hardware has to offer
and maybe a Private Jet. Like Grandad's. Only
minus Grandad. The girls at the airport treat
me a mischief. I know her type, they say.
Unaware of my ability to hear, never merely
thought, But any Human voice, over decimals.
Why may she never piss off to the chartered
end.??? (B)'itch's the likes of she usually fly
private anyway, I heard them say, as I walk
sadly away ashamed in lieu of management.
They, Unaware that in spite of my attire, my
good posture, and the great love I hold in
upkeep of my appearance, that I, at present,
may ill- afford such luxuries. I wanted to ask
for a lift to New York City atop one of
Napoleon's mighty Steeds. To Shake Shack. I
have never been. I am starving. Drooling over
Pinterest photos, and the want of that
delightful looking milkshake. Starving. I feel

such discomfort in this dirty world. Is there no one willing to help me?. Never one magic pill to soothe me or cloud thine eyes. Never see quite so much more than the (average) person .... I fear not. No one, just me. And my undying need for that Loopy loop up a ramp, in a lonely container filled ship yard in a 2013 Hunter Green John Cooper Works Mini Countryman with the white top, (Had I possessed One of my own). A White Number (9) on both doors. Equipped with 19" Black Double Spoked wheels. "I saw that one on YouTube", she said. My Third grade Math's Professor, Mrs. Beezio, seated perfectly (beltless), how shameful now damn near Octogenarian. Shotgun and gagged, though I shan't warn her. "The old Bitch", she growled. Should she be unfortunate enough to after such a long while hold life's breath, before clowning my religion, my beliefs, about a classroom devoured by laughter, be -forged the youngest of un-knowers. And what is alive. Why do we wish Death on our enemies?, It simply frees them. Let them stay and suffer with me, I often ponder. The broken hearted? The Dead too, wore hearts a-blazed. Their lives are over now. Were past, bruised, beating chest muscles a waste of time? Did it really matter?.

Does it still ? "Or should we even bother to Love", she asked. Have you an inkling,, the aagony of living in a world, full of Idiots. Agony with (2) small a's. (A speed reader with no arms makes an ill page turner.):©2014. "Ha, ha, ha, ridiculous", she said. Never knowing is never dumb, I explained. (Dummy), I think quietly.. Hee hee, laughed thine separate me. Another one leaving me to fend for self. Same as the others. Want, Pain, Need, Heartbreak even Silence. I stand amongst you. My left hand in full gripped Fear. Laughter stamped, snug under the soul of my now bloodied right foot. Laughing loudly, but only at myself. "Envy the dreamer", I shout, smiling, though in more pain than Isabel. In a world pretending to care, Gripped by a h@ll, with hands larger than any life imaginable. Dead or Dying. Alone, due to uncaring souls. Already Dead, amongst thy same uncaring souls,. I fester faster now. As many thoughts turn to rule, destruction. H@te, for anger never shown. And what I should have, would have done, lay dormant. Thoust who would have heard, have either forgotten or forgiven me. Having moved on. Whilst I lay filthy in a puddle of past desire never fulfilled. I Die. O Rotting Brain covet thy sole. Too heavy in despair,. Can't turn it off, Can't make it stop, The sounds grow louder, I plead. "Block", even throw up hands maternal, physical. What is she doing? I expect them to say, but no one is watching. Alone. Alone, I fight them. One after the other, comparing it long side a song stuck in my head. A song heard in over a fortnight, fresh. Playing over and over the same chorus. Still I scream, but cannot. I have since learned to scream where my childhood has left me breathless. Now my recipients of breath have all left. Stand tall (thine) enemy and forgive me. Then greet me in sorrow. Your out stretched hand at my stained, paint chipped door. A door left more times than less. Not I have passed through decades before, never to return. Still I lay here. Weep after weep. Stone after stone. My unheard Heart, shattered time and again. My sorrow weekend, hast me. YES, HAST. My body hung trunk over priciest of clothing. A mere front, as I trot, full of despair and torment. The anger. It is that very anger which gets me. Bursting fourth, ready to explode. Taking with it, thy beauty and perfect skin. O what a Lovely mess I shall make splattered on the walls of Gahenna. (GEHENNA):GREEK; meaning, (H@LL). (or Fires of). (H@LL): meaning; Eternal Life. In All Languages. My thoughts, nothing less than my own shit filled vomit and brittle hair. The exhausting need to care for, then nourish. Others do it. Yet the chained ankle'd fear pulls me tighter with age. Leaving me listless in body. "All I want is my own", she repeats. So that I may no longer beg. My high horse, cut short at the knee. Dropping me, then writhing in pain, as his own life slip silently away. Leaving nothing but the shell of where I have once ridden. "O why may I never escape this place", she asked screaming. Her hands remain cupped, fingers curled. "Clean". "Clean", she cried, collapsed on bloodied knee. (Automysophobia): The Fear of Being Dirty. "The Old opening through the alley, where I use to live" she said. The path leading out. If I could only make it to the end where wild roses grow, obscuring broken pebbles of the oncoming road." I am there", she said. I am there, I can see it. "NO", she screamed, "NEVER". Shaking the earth and all who possess her. Had it never been for the fact I am the sole owner of her presents. "Trapped", she said. Her hair and tattered white gown, now souled in fear, menstrual blood and soot. Release me. "I must leave them", she said. I hold much importance, little solace. Not I have one friend, nor reminder? Sept the Ghost of friend past who make-eth quietly my comfort. Offering shelter in a world familiar to my own, or one once shared. I visit, yet never stay. I feel love, then leave it awakened. Bound for this is my home. A home bent on the betterment of its self. Though left in my hands shan't see light. There is no help. I mean No Real Help. And without Daddy's donations may never bridge the gap between here and the Swiss Alps ever again. No one cares. This shit faced, every man for himself coalition of wolves is a game and I am losing in a mad rush to prevent thy womb falling alongside. "No", she muttered. "They must prosper through phlegm and loathing", she cried, reaching for my pant leg as her right cheek slowly connect to an icy, white, marbled floor, tucking her calves and dirty feet neatly beneath her. "I have lost control", she cried, sniff, snot, as slob riddled her hair, now wet dripped with cold sweat and fever. She desires my help, though she may never see me. I would cradle her, though she may never feel my arm's caress. A pat on the back, my short offering to a selfless, ruined by life soul and the cold hand-ed, left turned over the shoulder Mother, who in ailing state, just assured attest soiled pants in view of her older Brother, than descend to a discreet showing of hands for a mere chit of a girl. "You remember that day"?, she asked. "All I ever wanted is to be clean", she said. Clean, Happy, Healthy. Safe, she continued. My offspring and theirs in like. One wish, when others require three. But the Genies never appeared. I have waited, as my wait shall surpass food and shelter. The water of life flow downward past my door never catching my foot to wet even a big toe, as I yearn to leap, never leaving the ground. "I try", she screamed. I try till the whole of the night, then closing my shutters for the only peace known. Then awaken a day new to try once more, but nothing. I may try no more. My bones, now weakened from the fall of my dying bell shaped heart with its lousy, one horsed beat, set in a once, one horsed town now destined for fame. Most in like, yet set aside for those not of my kind. "I built this town", she sang, in an absolute un-control or concern for her own off putting Pseudoptyalsm, that lessen my concern or stomach for gaze in her direction. (PSEUDOPTYALISM): Ptyalism, a condition characterized by the excessive flow of saliva, also referred to as hyper salivation. Or (False Ptyalism): The release of excess saliva accumulated in the oral cavity. Common, mainly in Dogs and Men of Great Knowledge. A constant production secreted into the oral cavity from the salivary glands, onto the floor, and not inches from my Ann Demeulemeester Triple Lace Boots. (Rhypophobia): The Fear of Filth. "Your vanity precedes you", she pronounces, looking unappreciatively, upward me in haste. "Why must I touch, then touch again", she growled, repeatedly in a room now left vacant by the last remaining evils, sept for she and myself. (OCD):Obsessive Compulsive Disorder. I must be mad. I Must Be Mad. "I want to go and take Him with me", she cried pitifully. He deserves better. Our bowels fill with no pot. Our stomachs yearn, minus a stove. As I lay sick, choking on common comfort, stuck at the back of my throat. Disabling life giving breath needed to save our lives. Why have they yet to retrieve me? My time here has spent. Why abandon me with nothing more than a tobacco wrapped dream and little else to comfort me. The beginning of Noon Prayer hours and none after (30), turn swiftly through my head though I, at this very moment, remain forever ready. Nothing else to look forward to or delight me more than a lung full of immune weakening smoke filled chest tightening breath. (9) tokes, now (8)...(7) to follow the first of January, eventually, non. Leaving me with nothing, sept for the Cancer. I want it now, I cannot wait. Why must a minute last (2) or (3) when others wait (1). I wait, shaking. But like I always say, (A pencil is only good till the eraser wares): © 2014. I stand alone. Unknowing, amongst those who know exactly what the day shall bring. Where, what is to be consumed. Relief, cleansing, rest. How they shall commute. Who awaits they're arrival. What tomorrow shall hope to bring. How and when demands shall be, or hope to be met. The friendly faces connected and how they want to believe is felt about them. I move silently amongst them. Unseen, confused, and unwanted, in a haze of perfection. And they want to be like me? "WOW", I witnessed one women to say to another, while pointing in my direction. "I know she's happy". Huh. Is she Bloody joking, I thought. I simply smiled in another direction. We should never judge. Or am I wrong for judging. The unhappy seem happy, while I seem all together put. Sadness, hopelessness, Fear. Stealthy, silent creatures, they are. Moving about our souls. Clinging to us like parasites. Diseases, undetected by light and Credit Ratings. Perhaps had we known we were one. We,, all one, none would judge. One being in Billions of tiny bodies. Spread out across the Earth and other galaxies like a plague. The fisherman, the fool. The police officer, the life splitter. The King, the sheltered. The Whore, the giver. The so called House Wife, the worrier. The Billionaire, the Faith spoiler. All one, with such lessons to learn, allow envy to rule. "I walk my path separately, as need be", she said, I always have. If we are one, never we may see nor believe. One being, separated. One soul, many paths, is the reason man destroys man, destroying himself. Had we learned this long before we learned trust? But there is none, never knowing, we do not know. ©2014. I now recall. The whole of my schooling, forgotten. It is all coming back to me. If I could only make them understand. But my human side wants what it cannot have. And such information would bring about World corruption, even on a good day. A day when all is made known. One out of (6), or (7) Billion would comprehend, the rest in Mass Hysteria. "Humans un-knowingly shun the love of one another", she said. It has never been my calling to warn them. I am No Saint, No Jesus, No Muhammed. I would simply find myself crushed and trampled in the great rush for Equality. A greasy stain left for a cleaner like mine. And though well paid for his services, place himself beneath the Rich, but even higher above me, with no knowledge of same. We remain separated, merely by lack of such knowledge. (Let him walk his path and never envy him. For he is you): ©2009. Part of you, but never the part you wish to prosper. You want to do it. Why not me, Why him, you cry. (If you see it, you too were there. If you hear it, feel it, touch it, witness it, It is yours): ©2014. And you lack energy, plus the guts to admit that someone did it so you would never haf to. Yes Haf. The world has become one big sloppy bum. The common, uneducated man's instinct tells him that a women who never keeps her body clean and trim of floppy bits, holds little or no intelligence. Leaving little effort for Coition, he gravitates towards her type. After all, who has time to buy flowers, candy, get to know someone, respect them, or even ask a name, before grossly impressing himself upon. When his main goal is Ball greasing. (COITION):The act of sexual procreation, between a Man and a Woman. (PROCREATION):To produce offspring or reproduce. I envy the writers who speak proudly of Death. One Author wrote about how she had been passed so long, that her

Children were no longer her own. Shall our realities play out in such a manner? Or may I pass on, then return when there time is up. Grasping their hands. Leading them to the safety and securities of a warm home somewhere. Then it is there where we may forever await arrival, the rest. Wrapped in the understanding of life, now it has done. May we Laff, yes laff at the times we believe to have felt pain, sadness, hurt. "Wow", we shall all say in unison, as our voices have now become one., " Is this a joke"? she asks, has this all been a quiz? How dare they. The off-handed writer, thinking deep. As deep as I dare. When I pride myself so, on the depths of thinking deeper than others, yet they have probed deeper. Contradiction. Have I not just explained how we are all one. (LOL). Dear Bibliobibuli, you MUST learn to catch such things. (Bibliobibuli): One who Reads Too Much. "And though desperately hoping our paths are never connected", I continue. Can bet countless on one man's Euros, they, at this very moment have captured, then released my sharp warmth. The thoughts were mine. I would have gotten there, given time, but I am slow. Slower than most, only light years ahead. Plus I am forbidden to reveal all and shall remain as such. I remember, one March morning, having just given birth to my eldest child. (Fell Ill), on uncaring hands. And as I walk through that valley of the shadow of Death. A field of white poppies, towards that large swing that hang still, unaffected by the wind. Stemming from a tall Oak. The tallest, as I to my own amazement remain un-effected by my Megalophobic state. My pain lessened. Reaching for total relief of never returning, as I endure a sharpness towards the left of my Cleft AL Horizon, returning me. Reminding me that my time is not of yet. A nine gauge in the backside by Doc herself. " We almost lost you", she said smiling and rustling her hand atop of my head. (CLEFTAL HORIZON): The Intergluteal Cleft, or BUTT CRACK. By now you are thinking; Who does this Bitch think she is? And if there ARE others such as herself,,, well. Ahh, but I have since met a man, A blind man. Born without sight, who may describe, in detail my very field, my very poppies, in white, and my very swing, hanging from that very Oak, whilst having a near death experience such as mine. Now, decades later, the escape hatch opens. Through the passage I could see all fear diminished. I no longer belonged to this world, did not want to, and wondered why I either had never seen this prior, or why I have devoted a majority of my time here to start. You may go now, a voice said. Though I heard nothing as I moved among the living, unseen, as if to float. I knew I would forget all about this world and all it lay before me. Then I remembered I would forget you. (YOU): PLURAL,. You are Plural. (YALL?): A short cut brought about by the Lazy. Perhaps I should entitle this book YOU ARE PLURAL. YOU: Meaning, EVERYONE. My Children and Grandchildren, equaling my World. Had I never been myself all may have been right as rain. Knowing myself, I would remain aware of the very thing that I am forgetting. I am not ready to forget you. If I leave this World now, shall you remain?, How then, am I to be Happy times Free. Totally forget? An ever so exhausting encounter. Scary, yet I indeed fancied the off. To take me, unloading my body, there lifeless for all to wonder. The feeling were great and horrible. I see your faces, fading, as I forgot who you were. "No", she said, silently among strangers in a cloud of doubt, regret, sadness, solitude. All the while dreading the long, Lonely haul home." I shall, one day leave them here. "Not of yet", I spirt at a volume to startle a sales girl, standing at the till. "NEXT", she shouted. And with such promising destination, decided to wait. Why did I bring them here? Or more to the point. I Brought Them Here. Were it to drop them off. To fend for self? Sad. Or would they remain. Has this too been a test? Are they un- real? A figment of my imagination? My very own Children? There Children? Shall they diminish alongside me? Along with a World I once thought to be mine? Do I (haf) to leave them at all. Is this restitution, or worse than the fact of leaving them in a World of which I may never return? "I nearly left that time", she screamed. I nearly left. "How I long for the walk beside them", she said. Die next to them in laughter. My eyelids heaviest in view of their smiling safe, happy, healthy, secure, warm, well- fed faces. Tucked in and alive. Praying. "There is no such thing as the Genius and My foot hurts Singular", she shouts. (DAVID NIVEN): March 1st,1910-July 21st,1983. An English Actor Popular in Europe as well as the States for his Roles in The Pink Panther, and Around The World in (80) Days. A Novelist. The Moons a balloon (One of my Faves). "You Lied to me", she screeched, leaping towards me in anger nearly to slice me on sharpened nails had it never been for the chains which bind her. "You have been lying from the start", she said, now returning to her rightful place on the floor.. I am not Gorgeous, not Beautiful. It has all been a line. A catch phrase. "You say it to everyone", her voice withered in deceit. "Oh how thou hast lov-ed thee", she did spout proudly as to a hushed audience. With all my heart, I loved you. But alas, I have never been enough, she cried, as she once again turns her back to me. I shall never, to this very day, fully comprehend, dissect to whom she is referred. A past Lover, perhaps? One more figment of her imagination? Her Mother? I doubt this very much. Her father?,,, A common oligarch, with pockets as deep as the sea, and the lock on them tighter than a Brown egg, Cornstarch home facial in full view of the sun in (90) degree weather. Though anything I fancied were to be mine and had better be of top quality. Give It To Her. THEN SHE IS TO HAVE IT. Daddy would often say. At The Double, snappy now about it, He'd growl. Wrap it, make a pretty parcel. While he, In exile to Geneva in order to avoid all circumstance of Her Mother? Russian Woman. A retired Restaurant Critic. Now a year or so past Octogenarian, who lay and wait of her angels. Releasing too, her tortured soul, freeing this poor girl, or maybe just to show up and rate the salad cream.

(OCTOGENERIAN):Noun; One between (80) and (89) years of age. No one? Or am I the one to whom she is referring. Who's to know, when only half eyed. "She only gives you half eye anyway", relayed my 3rd eldest sister to my Father, regarding my shyness. Yes, I thought. My face stamped with a revenge filled smile. Relay this to the man. The man who has only known me the whole of my life. Where it never, his distrust, abuse, over power-ment and rage, which has seen me safely to this point and time? By all means, my girl, tell him, Now tell him again. This Life. What a life I have lead. (a devil) may cry, bent, Praying towards the East, would he the balls to seek such direction. "Take from me these shoes", he cries. Would he were allowed my very presence. I may no longer walk in them. For my foot, too, hurts, Singular. This life is shit. How dare I release, the thickening waters of birth, set fourth, my offspring and ask them to take in like, a shit housed World of ill repute, and no remorse. "How dare I", she cried, How dare I. (THIS LIFE):A book by Sydney Poitier. (Sydney Poitier): KBE; Bahamian- American actor, Author, Film Director. (No association).

(And no association with that which I have stated prior). A life, where blood is foreign. Blood does not understand, may never try. Disgust, is blood relation. How do I love a man, who in October of (81), an (11) year old me, first got her Period. But I do. Were forced, kept in hand, a bottle of spray cleanser and a rag, called upon each time Dear Old Daddy, spotted a scarlet spec. On more than one occasion,, it turned out to be paint or nail varnish. But never the matter, I lay blame. "May I never embarrass one of my Children in such manner", I asked, kneeled East. Oh, said mother, How Terrible. Now in her old and often imitated demented state. You were just as bad, You feeble old trout, I wish to say, but shan't. I am working towards forgiveness, but though it wrong of any man, I never forget, and this is one of those days. I can recall freighting the old Mare, as I do apologize most strongly. Believing she were speaking with me. Found herself in full frontal conversation with..... wait, I had better pause at this very point until my Son returns before continuing. I feel them, surging round. Even now, I have deceived you by waiting on his return before writing just that bit as well. Mother, Bless Her, has had a conversation with, who she found belief to be me. I, having no knowledge of their encounter, felt no puzzlement when Mother, in slackened state, conveyed to me "THEN YOU THRU-UP UR ARMS AND SAID, SHE HAS TATTOOS, I HAVE NON", revealing bare arms. But Mother had never spoken to me beforehand. Now I shiver in fear, at the fact that SHE, must be about. Dear MUM had been using her old adages on non-other than, YOU HAVE GUESSED CORRECTLY. "It is I", she said. You assumed you were speaking to the coward. "She has tattoos", she said lifting her arms. I keep repeating the phrase over and over, as I cannot help but laugh. To Mothers surprise and everyone who sail in her, now finds she is speechless in a strange place. "Silence", she told me, as I head back to yours. Ha Ha,, we did laff. (LAFF) "You shall have little more trouble out of her", she said. The poor old thing. And until this very day, she remains ever so Silent in my path. But shall I speak of this twice?, You Bet. (3) times the least amount at best. Repetition is king and I have sat on that throne long before his Coronation. (REPETITION, THE WAY IN WHICH WE LEARN). REPETITION: 1.the action of repeating something that has already been said or written. (OXFORD DICTIONARIES). You must try and understand. I lay witness to Mothers Evil. I had been warned, on many occasion, yet suppressed the attempt to delve further. Till that slumber, The Proof. A dream. My dreams hold truths, never your regular, held in the back of the mind stuff. More to the point, what I can only see during a place past conscience. And there she were. The lone H@te, Vile, never Believing anything I say look, that she most harbored for me. No skin, but hair. Staring me down, as she often had, following a complaint of pain, or a gasp of missed breath, owing to my breathing problem. Yet any lie or exaggeration grabbed her full attention. How twisted. Any grasp towards health nor healing, ignored. Sent to a place of untruths or impossibilities. The cold, almost sure of me lying look on her resent - filled face, locked to my eyes as that of a portrait which follows you around the room. Ugly, terrifying eyes. Hers. The ones I remember over Decades of hurt and a feelings of non-escape. The ones she has to this very day. Sick. Sick, incurable, by any amount of Lithium injected. With more white than her usual brown. The eyes of Horror. Hhorror, with a Capital and small (h). For one's own child? I am unable to look away, though feeling completely unsafe. As I walked through our old passage to the front sitting room where she stood. I could now see that she had been sliced in half. Right down the middle, yet jagged. Like a purposely torn page or un wanted bill. Did this convey that the woman were but half Evil? Maybe her other half, if I cared to locate, could be somewhere lost and in need of some assistance. Searching, begging for help. Pleading innocence. The halfhearted beast filled with the Love she had shown me. As Mother displayed nothing but an oven's warmth of care for me 40% of our time together. But I would never lift a thumb to help would I to happen upon the retched half sided filth. "Had I known, would I have let her harm you?", I she said. In a World of Saints and Sinners, may none of ye statue-ed stone release to bludgeon thee before striking? "Who?", she asked. Who would have suspected a tiniest of shaken'd girl? What strength to have done such things. "Could never have been her", they would say. Would thou have freed me. Would thy have lived past solitude in these chambers? With nothing, only less nothing than nothing's past,. Or the nothing I feel now, never knowing. We are always given the benefit. "I am a believer", she sang. I am a Believer. For an ever in it shall I hold. Do not cry, they told me "DO NOT CRY", in higher note she sang. Her hands cuffed to the sky in Prayer. Do not cry, for you may never forsake him. It were the first time I am a witness to tears of joy on such a stained smile. A new experience for one such as I, myself. Her dirty face, in such a dirty dress, on such a clean floor made dirty by such. (Mysophobia): Fear of Dirt, Germs. And where are we going with this story? Well the truth is like that. Not merely this one. No, my dear. She is but a mere trifle. Trust me, I have met them all. From the Tooth Fairy, to Miss-carry. (THE TOOTH FAIRY): Folklore states that when a child loses a tooth they must place it under their pillow before bedtime. The fairy will then replace it with a small fortune. About .25₱, to be exact. Rubbish. My number (34). Right hand bottom. Wisdom Tooth. Root of all evil, as my complaining ware thin, a wall of stone and brick, laced between night and day, outdoors and sheltered places. While I, a Mother to most, Grandmother to some. And in my tween 40's, shout and shun pain, or as I say, "You could shoot me in it and it shall never compare". Crouched in pain and a half bottle of Red. Posted ever so neatly between sleep and nod, hear a tapping, a thump. My shoulder warn raw, as you lean upon it, O tiny one. With tiny feet, tiny wings, and dressed as though you have dressed yourself for the first time. For a split second never, I see her. Around to my face, she is now posed. Her finger, never leaving my jaw, baring the face of the old, in tiny pink clothing. "I thought you were a child", I said. "I thought you were an adult", her sharp Whitty reply. A silent speech, heard only by myself and most like me. As she, along with the pain, have now vanished. Away with my tooth. Leaving never a penny for my thoughts. Merely a great belief of no one who may hold in trust such a tale, nor believe me. Vampires, Werewolves, The Extraordinary. (Miss-Carry): The Taker of Miss-carried Children. A Worldly one of sorts. Draped in Black. Followed in hoards, by tramples of unpitter-ed pattered feet and no womb. OOOOwwww. Thy pain is all too real, as I wiggle and twist, in search of a comfortable path past her probing digits, plunged deeply to my stomach. The angered, tickled, ever so escape needing pain. Searching, searching again, finding nothing. Away. Her disappointment." It twere only gas, you silly Sassenach," I said repeatedly and to my own surprise, in a well-rounded Irish lit. "I Twernt pregnant". The Ware wolf, (LUPIN), whose mother indulged. The Blood Sucker whose Mother restrained. A matter of class? I have since met a man from different Worlds who think, we, Bar-Barrack, merely for the fact that we eat. Consume?" Why?", he asked, must you inhale, then exhale so swiftly, to un- allow nutrients from your air the nourishment of your bloodstream. Why the very act of such behavior, causes you to crave the flesh of animals along with such beautiful vegetation? All real. Nothing imagined, Nothing made up. (The Mind does not, nor has it the ability to Create, but only the ability to realize); ©2010. Being that there is no such thing.????? Careful how we use such words. Everything Exist. Or have I misspelled it? The mind does not create it only realizes; ©2009. Is what SHE, meant in her Philosophy. The human mind may never, nor has the ability to conceive actual truth. In layman's term, think IT, and IT may well be. In the early 70's, the cell phone, as we now know it, has never been wwidely distributed. (wwidely, with 2 small double v's). Yet the technology wash around us, (we). Waiting, as I too, wait to be discovered. However fowl or distorted. Careful what you dream my girl. "How I want so desperately to do

SOMETHING", she said. While I, the normalcy seeker, need only what others take so needlessly for granted, as I have stated prior. And once all are obtained, what left have we to shed a tear. The health of our Loved Ones? A Prayer shall suffice. A smear of black coal. Rouge drippings for ones face on the occasional outing. Nothing fancy or overpriced, when you are as talented as such. Just the needed. And one may never use the word H"@Te,... Why the very divulger of such a word as it stands, may well age thy skin. Rotting the soul. As in a lie or thievery. Now my inconsolable soul is needed. Needing, as it sought, once more, the solace of absolute something-ness. Lost in a crowded field, with no one to hold its hand. While others clutched tighter. Watching as the sun set in its ways. A mere copy, as it has night after night and nights before this. "What am I to do now", she said, looking indirectly up at me. But I have no response. I too, have come in search of an answer. And if you are my one hope, I Deem myself, Dammed For All Eternity. "Why leave me here"?, she has asked, time and again. What am I to do? My contribution? "I am restraining them", she said, as she has on many occasion. Holding them back. Without me, the gates shall open. Setting forth the winds of change. Nourishing the ground where I once laid, pity filled, blocking the sun. "Hindering new growth", she said. What torments me upon my wake and Death, worries me not, the fact my name Un-Appears on Forbes list of World's Richest Women. More only, the fact that School-aged Children, may never the chance, study my life in History Books. "Few, ever set an eye upon me", she explained. The simple, around about their perfect lives in haste. An in and out situation, with no showable, (Seeable) worry. And when seen as such, I may approach, comfort and ease you. For I am no such perfect. Refusing upon myself, your remark of such. "We are Alien", she spat. As new bloods form and secretion demolish any hopes of cleansing that stain. I am getting worse, you know. Soon I shall forget, but until that day, shall remain un-ready. Such an occurrence pains me, how my remembrance, coupled with how I may somehow never care, collide head on like the line between love and ,,,, Well.... (LOVE):noun; Dictionary.com describes it as: A Profoundly, Tender, and Passionate Affection for another Person. A feeling of warm personal attachment or deep affection as for a Parent, Child, or Friend. I describe it as: Verb; Something I do or give with no remittance. Though I use the term incorrectly. The Long distance, with little or no confirmation of return. If you expand your brain, Love can mean lots of things and everything. To some, very little. To a chosen few, nothing at all. (REMITTANCE): I Shan't define it. Money is Vulgar. A mere deterrent from GOD. (Deterrent): Something which discourages or is intended to distract from doing something else. Fear, Power, the (2) Greatest Sins of Man. Prayer, our one gift. Given, rarely used. (Believe in all, Practice few); ©2010. "Beaten down by my profound loneliness", she said. Beaten down by it. How does one trust anew, or imagine being with another. Does Love simply fade", she cried." No", she said, Never for me. Does one forget the feelings or the person. How does one fathom another. How does one seek returned happiness, alongside assurance of unhappiness. Again. An ever repeated cycle. A large Gin and laughter with a pain chaser. I Go Alone, Eat, Drink Alone, Leave Alone , Arrive Home, Alone, Fall asleep. Alone. Where does thou stand, others such as myself ? Could I stand them, Look them in the eye. Stomach them, or merely envy them? There would haf to, yes, Haf, to be others. (1 GOD). (2) or more of everything else) ©2009. She would always say. But none my age and years with nothing or no one, I assure you. It is pathetic how I move about, wishing, hoping, pleading, then false forgiving. "What Now"?, she asked. When the wishing and hoping have now left me. Why must I be condemned to live while others die. The taking of my own life will leave, yet another space to fill, with bloodied tears and complaints of why I did such ,,,when others never. Look at them all. Living, whilst I lie here, cold, I say. Why must my time move ever so slowly? (1) minute? (5) In my world. Less I am tardy a minute last a millisecond. Skipping an hour. As I am sat alone, in hopes of (30) pills ingested. Sending me. Leaving questions, only by a letter left reading. (I grow weary of my Lone Confinement). Loneliness is an awful place. Heavy, yet free. With the surprising twist of, No One To Tell. Just me. The Other me. My Handbag, Clothes and Shoes. Death Report: Loneliness. Headlines read;,,, "Died of Loneliness"?. My supposed Suicide to Farewell letter, Published for all to see, simply reads;

(And I pity the day, Bless Her. For I shall once again waste her time, the poor thing. I have nothing to offer you, My Dear Morning, Noon and Night. No point in showing your faces. You shall stand hopeless, as I watch you go by with no name, no meaning, no outcome. So stand and watch me in wonder, Dear Confusion and Impatience,. Wishing you had graced another).

And yet I remember, another therapist, who has yet to defined my fears. "I have been seeing him for (2) years", she cried, looking down at an empty hand, as to read from a letter or book. "ENUFF", I shout. She ignores me, continuing on. He still has no idea or any medical terms for my phobias. Shrugs his shoulders like the rest when asked. My med keeps him in the new Auto. Keeps him in Glass houses. My fear of Trains, ?

" What is that", he asked in amazement. (Siderodromophobia). I had to research my own fears,????. Where is my Money. Where is my Bloody Money, she cried. Money is Vulgar, you said. Yet I live in a home with no kitchen or (loo), on account of bad pipe? No. Tis my fear of Wet Wall. Maybe medical shall pay me, sense I have spent so much effort in diagnosis. My fear of large objects, what's that, I asked. Still he has no known cure nor knowledge of such illness out of context or meaning thereof.

(Megalophobia). (Megalo): GREEK; meaning Large. Countless others. Repetition. My (PANOPHOBIA): The fear of everything. He simply grins, prescribes pills, and in less than (5) minutes I am set on my way. Released back into the world, alone. "ENUFF", I say, once more. There shall be no more talk of Shrinks. No more talk of Fear. No longer shall I endure what the World owes you. Have I not stood, long and fast? Have never I stood, Standing, for years on end. As I, in complete patience, lend an unclosed ear on your ills?. "No More",, I shout. No longer, shall you complain of pee and where it lands. For decades now, I have lay witness as you splatter, never one drop, upon an already, h@ll fated floor. No more, shall you speak of hot plates and dis-repair fallen work spaces on which to prepare meals. Meals, that are devoured in seconds before my very eyes. Have you not Dinned sufficient? Such a coveted frock, which you have so perfectly destroyed. Is it not an Armani Original? Have you not, a warm dark space to dream? While I, who care so dearly for you, remain forever sleepless. Forever awake? Jesus has, what your beloved, Dis-believer, deemed as Nothing. Yet remained steadfast in Prayer. While you speak more of the Disbeliever before declaring, you, yourself as one. Disbelieve, is to judge. Disbelieve, is to look down upon. (But seek ye first the Kingdom of GOD, and his righteousness and all these things shall be added unto you.)- Mathew 6:33. O My Dear Doc now sits, (1000's) of pounds Richer," she continues, in such a manner to concede my word thin to vapor on release. " I too, continue my search for answers", my response. And a pot to piss in. "Look", she said reaching into her bosom. I have (1€), One Euro. "It should be against, SOME law to diagnose a person with Cancer", she says, changing the subject midstream as always.. The moment you hear such a word, STRESS, triggers the dying process. Kills you. I can go about my marry life, with the Cancer. Living happily and free. Then,,,, The moment I seek advice of, (sed) Physician,, months, sometimes, weeks, Days later, I am Dead.? It were never the Cancer, more the Diagnosis. Words prey heavily, the air in which we breathe. If we were abashed to see them, we would swat them like flies from festering meat. (ABASHED)? LOL. Kick them aside like a lazy Saturday afternoon, when no one on Earth craves the laundry. A word such as Cancer, is in itself, is no less a Cancer. (Cancer): Cancer is a group of diseases involving abnormal cell growth with the potential to invade or spread to other parts of the body. (WIKIPEDIA). What we speak, grow rapid. Careful, what we speak, for WORD, is magic.; ©2016. Stress of Knowing. Anticipation. Thinking, I am going to die. Have you never noticed?. You hear it time and again. So and So passes on a mere (x) amount of weeks after being diagnosed. AFTER?,, AFTER,, never before, behind diagnosis. The stress of knowing.???? If ,,, you concentrate hard (enuff), on any one thing, it may happen. Magic. Dying is the biggest event in our lives. The most beautiful, most exciting thing to ever happen to the whole of we. The very reason we all rise from our slumber. Believe it or not, dying is the most important event of our lives. The single, Greatest achievement, is Death. Like dressing for the Oscars. You spend the whole of your lives preparing for that one slip of a moment when you feel nothing. Regardless of how the papers print it, you feel nothing. No gun shot. No fall. No loud Bang. No plane crash. No loud clap, no clatter. Nothing. No more than a slight flutter. Imagine your jacket sleeve caught on a hook, then someone lifts it from the hook. How Beautiful a feeling. Far more important than any and everything. Most think it finance, or food. We wait our entire lives, for that very moment when we expect to hear the final explosion, followed by great pain and sorrow. Unable to scream, think. Dark nothingness? Forever? How could such a thing imaginable ever be as so. If we think now, we shall go on. Thinking. If we are reborn, we shall go on. Never the nothingness of Death, or so we have been led to believe, Death. If you think now, where shall your thoughts go after Death? On. If we were to begin a journey on the great dark nothing, when would it end? However long the Nothing last. There would come a time when you would ask, ok, when does this nothing end, I am terribly bored with it. "How I longed to find my soul-less body dragged, screaming onto an old dirty city transport, filled with the ugliness of souls in remembrances", she states proudly, smiling. People-less creatures in tattered, torn, black clothing. Begging Forgiveness. For one more chance. Chained to their seats, crying. Their unwashed Hair, standing on edge and un-shaven. Then with a great, Horrifying roar of the engine, at the speed of light, the world stops, as we take off, now faster. Faster. Up ahead the road opens, like a mouth full of un- brushed jagged teeth.

And in a flying haste, we are eaten up. Devoured by that road. And as we descend to a h@ll, the screams grow even louder and I am Terrified longing for the security of family and humble homes. Down, down, and I am terrified, but never alone. Never to be seen again, as we are swallowed up by the ground and her sharp witted teeth. But alas, our final scene may never play out in such a manner. The very reason why Great thinkers achieve. Concentration. From me to my fellow Clairvoyant. The very thought has now changed all, has it not ? Much like the Euro. Now, I say, In order to answer your question, I first must explain to you. Educate you on your reasoning of such a question. You underestimate the Power of ONE. Never,,,, under- estimate the power of $1.00, (1) euro, ETC. 1 Dollar changes everything. (I only have one dollar). If you had (9,999)€ ,, look at this number. Rounds and sticks. An open space, a closed space. A secure, warm, closed in space. A stick, a passage leading out, when required. Everything it needs to be happy. Lots of friends. Now add the Euro, or Dollar, whatever.

9,999

  + 1

10,000

Now what have you? One lonely you and a bunch of closed in holes with no out, no air holes. That (1) Dollar has now changed your entire World. Never underestimate the power of (1). Same as the diagnosis. There (9,999) is, strolling along, happily enjoying himself. Then after the (1) thing you all fear most is introduced. The 1 thing, most important thing. The Hope of Death or (1)... Everything turned to Zero (A Not). Little else matters at this point. You are going to Die. Your mind is reminding you, I am alone, I am (1). (0,000), equals nothing. The mind starts a festering process. Since the Mind may never prosper from negative thought. And to fear Death is a Sin. Thee, YES, THEE most unavoidable... We rot from the Brain down. Lend me never, your Diagnosis. Allowing me to live my extra (9,999) days. If you tell me that I have Cancer, I may only live the 1... (0,000. zero equals nothing).

Daddy had survived, at aged (12), a shotgun blast to the abdomen. By aged (25), A shark attack. By (74), A chainsaw to the Femur. Countless assassination attempts throughout his life. Never to mention, a failed Abortion attempt by his very own Mother. Our own Mother unloaded (6) rounds from an old German Luger into his chest, whilst he stand before me. Pushing him into the next room. As I run to his aid, squinting for the sight of blood and shards of heart may abrupt, yet another fear to add to the long list, I find him upright, un-bloodied shirt, never a pain on his face. Gracefully, as always, stepping into his English Made Shoes. Retrieving his hat and coat, to drive himself to Hospital. Only part that stunned me about Daddy on this day, is that he normally has a driver.

He has, on more than one occasion (As Most May Have It), Cheated Death. NO SUCH THING. After being Diagnosed with Cancer, he telephoned to say, and I quote (Baby, I May Not Beat This One). END QUOTE. Two months later and I am touching his lifeless body. No Heart Beat. As we could always hear Daddy's Heart beat if we were in the room with him. If we could hear it, would he were not in the room, it may well have been wise to hide. Played It's Last Beat? That is all she wrote, as Daddy would often say. Yes. Only days prior, Daddy were to be seen, running, swimming, snooker, Golfing. A (91) year old man. NO MORE DIAGNOSIS. AND WHILE I HAVE YOUR ATTENTION:

The Russian European Rocket to Mars cost a whopping (9) Hundred Million, to check for life on Mars. Mars.???? What ,,,,?,,, Are we living in a B-Rated Sci-Fi now? The life here on Earth could use that (9) Hundred Million to improve itself. Maybe a class in how to mind our own BLOODY business to start. There are, currently, Women losing their Children to starvation, Here, on Earth. I may, or may never afford the laundry this fortnight. A mere £20, with drying. Oyster card fare to and from the matt, plus detergent, and I am left with just enough to feed and house a nations Hungry and Homeless, Save Fever Tree Tonic Water, Trade Stock at FTSE 100, Save countless Women from sex slave camps, provide adequate Health Care to those who lack. Negotiate, at least, part, of the cure for Aids, and Cancer. Never provide shoes for Children in parts of Africa, seeing as they neither need nor want them. Educate Teachers in the Art of

Education,... Cease the quiz of The Students
on what they know so that they may be
labeled, A,B,C,D,F people for the remainder of
their lives. Give them the answers, have them
write everything 10 times or more till it sticks
firmly to one or more Brain cells and let that be
that. Purchase a Home for me and my Son,
with a working Kitchen and Bath, a package of
peanut M&M's, AND A MUTHAFUCKING
MINI COUNTRYMAN. There you have it, 75%
of the Earth's problems, SOLVED,, for less than
(850) million Euro. Less we Leave money-
making Fads, such as Global Warming and The
Greening of our Lifestyles to whom hold more
Leisure, resulting from their own personal
(900) Million. We treat our fellow Earthlings as
if they were nothing. So why search for life
elsewhere? Perhaps, if found, they may never
submit to such tortures and Torments as WAR
and Welfare cuts. And since there is No
European Solution and definitely No US one.
Perhaps the (900) Million may possibly find
itself in use of locating one. Or at best, fund a
new wardrobe for the Worlds News teams. As
they sit pretty in front of camera, claiming that
one has been found. Methane? We have
Methane here, ON EARTH. Probably floating
in the Milk we serve our Children. Those of us

who may afford Real milk. Methane Gas is a Metabolic Byproduct of some Micro-Organisms, usually if there is no Oxygen present. "So, I assume they are searching for Martian Bovine", she said. That is about as silly as expecting good WIFI during Midday in China. No matter what part of the World you reside. Or Galaxy. Think, I said. Think. I may be no Steven Hawkins, but The human race, sure as fire, faces extinction. Never for lack of (Ana din), and (Nurofen). But do to loss of the obvious. Loss of brain power. We have lost our ability to think for ourselves. Take for instance, An episode of (Are You Being Served). The clock. As Mr. Granger, (Arthur Brough), assumed he had been made redundant. Mr. Grace, (Harold Bennet), who had originally never planned to attend the Anniversary Dinner, shows up, pretends to be senile by accepting the clock as if it were being granted to him. When in fact a man worth millions of Dollars, is in no way, an Idiot. In no way is he worth as much for being a dummy. Nor has he failed his math's. He, having been a Millionaire, never sleeps. For if he ever dared, Poor Dear, he would emerge from his night's slumber penniless. I assume he were at home going, over the figures, and as it seems, found he would fare, far better, in the long stretch financially, by keeping Mr. Grainger on for a few extra years. You must try and understand, once you gain financial power, you never want to lose it. One would die, sooner than face the return to poverty after a taste of life has been given. We must never watch tele. If so, we must learn from it. Use it as a thinking tool. Otherwise, it shall obtain its main purpose. To Keep (WE) Entertained, while the rest of the world turns around us. Keep us entertained, while the Big Money changes hands. You must think, walk, breathe. If you have, what you have been led to believe as, no money. Get up, go out. Walk not drive. Look. Think. Breathe, again. Breathe. In, now out. Imagine, We live in a world, on a planet, never falling off. Yes the World is round. Never in surface shape. Meaning everything is different every second of every second and different from itself indeed everywhere holding the same stress as itself in complete opposite of itself in likeness though completely different. " Have you not yet fallen off", she said, full of life and jumping. YET?, she repeats. Well worth the effort. But I pretended never to hear. Holey shit, how fascinating. This is real, or a dream. Either way, you experience it. Love. Love

leaving despair in a mind's rear view. Love.
Would you were to feel a love for everyone
you lay privy near, they would become ever so
beautiful to you. Sooner consider them your
type or no. When you make eye contact, you
become a part of that person's life. Love. We
have but one gift in life. Prayer. When Desire
leans forward, reach for Love. "Have never ye,
a great love towards me?", I asked, grasping
her shoulder to give her full on half eyed-ness.
Do you not Love me? I have been here since
day one. Watching, keeping you as safe as
possible. I wanted never, for you to work,
never to be friended. No mortgage. No
automobiles to harm you, harm others. For
Decades now, I have kept you warm, a full
Stomach. Safe from what others may feel. Yet
you look around and want what others believe
to possess. They are not happy. They are not
thinkers. You think. A thin wall of flesh,
blocking this happiness when you have such
an ability to see. You Think, for you may never
know such happiness. Neither have we come
to such a place in the hopes of finding
happiness. It would have been a frightful silly
of (WE). Success is a huge falsity. "We use a
beaker. "We are not nasty". Never nasty, she
says,??? Never hearing me. Turning away in

embarrassment. It is but all we have. Never NASTY? What have I told you? The whole of everything is nasty, or not. Depending on how we look at it.

QUESTION: WOULD YOU SOONER SHOOT YOURSELF OR BECOME DINNER FOR A HUNGRY LION?

ANSWER: THE LION.

QUESTION: REASON BEING?

ANSWER: THE LION MAY NEVER ATTACK ME. HE MAY NEVER EAT ME.

QUESTION: I BEG YOUR PARDON???????

ANSWER: IF I SHOOT MYSELF, UNDER ANY CIRCUMSTANCE, I AM COMMITTING SUICIDE. IF THE LION KILLS ME I AM MURDERED. NOW CHOOSE.

DO YOU FOLLOW?

IF I AM TO BE DESTROYED BY THIS LION, THE THOUGHT MAY WELL INDUCE CARDIAC ARREST. RENDERING ME DEAD, NEVER BY MY OWN HAND. IF I AM TO SURVIVE THE ATTACK, I SHALL FEEL

GREAT PAIN , NEVER DURING, BUT WELL
AFTER , AS I AM IN SHOCK, LIVING TO
TELL MY STORY. IF I AM TO BE EATEN BY
THE LION, ANGELS WILL SURELY TAKE
ME BEFORE I AM TO EXPERIENCE FEAR.

Daddy has SURVIVED a shotgun blast at age
(12), by a fellow dislodging his weapon into a
crowd of children, who he assumed were in
full attempt of siege on his home. Daddy,
having been pronounced, (D.O.A) by The Local
medical examiners. Stabilized, he, alongside
his fellows share in laughter at the news
clippings describing his Death. Believing that
he had, indeed murdered a child, the man
Hanged Himself. (Remember my contradiction
from icebreaker). Never attempt Suicide.
Imagine the conversation between this guy and
Daddy, the moment he realizes that Daddy has
lived a good (79) years after the event. But Let
us move on.

GET IT? IF NOT, YOU ARE SURELY NOT READY TO PERSURE MY PRIOR WRITINGS.

VERY WELL, THEN I SHALL PUT IT MORE SUCSINKLY. HERE ARE TWO MEN, IDENTICAL TO ONE ANOTHER,. SEPARATED BY THE MICRO THIN FIBER THAT IS HEAVEN AND A H@LL. BOTH MURDERED AT THE SAME TIME IN THE SAME MANNER.

H@*LL: WHY ARE YOU IN HEAVEN AND I AM HERE? WE ARE THE EXACT SAME .

Heaven: NOT EXACTLY, YOU SEE, I DID NOT FIGHT BACK.

NOW ARE YOU READY TO INDURE A FILTHY WORLD?

----

8 HOUR BREAK__ Good Morning

She has been asleep. "Sleep between the hours of (9) pm and (5) am, ONLY", she says, stretching. It is writing time again and I am cold. The air conditioning has played through the night. I could write you something and save the World, but it is never to be saved. I am not right, but I wish to be. I must tend to last night's pots and pans, but I wish never to do so. Eat between the hours of (3) and (6) pm, ONLY. You may, during this time, consume a small village of natives without gaining (1) pound.

I awaken very much full of anger. Angered, I am. Angered at the Death of my Father. Angered at those who have shown him the least amount of LOVE. Angered. My step sister has thought very little upon the Capital of a man she has despised from the beginning of the marriage. What shame I hold for you, Mother. She has never expected nor would she have expected my Father to leave a dime on her name. She DESPISED my Father. He, in return, Despised in like. If he lay before her, (2) pence, the brows raised could shatter windows from passing motorist causing a rethink on Big Brother's electrical end. You, she, and my younger Sister have had nothing but harsh words and thoughts for Daddy over the past (48) years. No, I shall never place upon a sheet of undying wood that she may hold in one hand an ounce of coin tainted words on ill effect my Fathers will. He merely left the youngest a dime to save face. VULTURISM;

The SIN shortly before GREED. I am in great need of a smoke, but the hour has yet to reach (6), as we Sprechen Deutsche, Speak English and Talk Italian.

So, as we have it, mother sells an Auto that is running, yet keeps two which are not. Compensating a man with tow. Moving them into a perfectly sound space which I had chosen for myself. Makes no sense, I said. You are in an evil and hateful mood today. No, I have merely grown weary of the pretense. The pretense of smiling. Saying what others wish to hear. My children may never grow up, she said. How then, Mother are we to grow up when only yesterday you, an (83) year old woman sat at the side of the bed cradling a newly purchased doll rocking, repeating the words, (They never let me have a doll when I were a child). How pathetic. I observe with less than 1 feeling of sorrow for her, merely pity. I have finished with sorrow. It has far past a waste of my time. You are feeling lazy and having a hate mother day, she said. No, I despise Mother every day, but the air has grown far too warm for pretending, as I crave the winter months. You and your brothers and sister H@te me. They H@te you on account you allowed Father to abuse them. They were never of his own **Blood**. And you, being so full of coward-ess, allowed such behavior to persist. Being of an age well past (60), I too pity the pair of them. The age in its self is punishment. I have seen far too often, Mother Nature's cruelties. I wish never to reach such an age. "Mother Nature and Her Lady Gravity are a Cruel, Evil, Lower Middle Classed BITCH", she said. And I would sooner die young then allow them grip upon me with their Poor Diction, Cheap Clothing and Vulgar use of punctuation. Nothing short of trash, the pair of them.

I have devoted an entire reading on past happenings to arrive at the point of, (WHO GIVES A SHIT). Perhaps my time is better spent on the envy of those with extra time to spend on the worry and torment of what others may or may never have done in the past. Or better still, what they are currently doing or thinking. As I now thank thy beloved Reader as he has grown alongside my feeble mindedness. We shall now proceed. I wish never to start the story anew. So ,,, let's move along, shall we.

WORDS AND PHRASES, THE LIKES OF WHICH
I WISH NEVER MORE TO ENCOUNTER;

PLUS SHIPPING AND HANDLING
DO THE MATH
WAKE UP AND SMELL THE COFFEE
D.I.Y
IT (WAS) HILARIOUS
BITCH (CONTRADICTION)
BITCHES
MY BITCH
YO BITCH
HA U DOIN
HAVE A BLESSED DAY
I'M BLESSED
DON'T CHALL WORK TOO HARD NA
MAKEUP DUPE
THANK YALL
BAD BITCH
BE BLESSED
AH-O-MEE-NO-HARM (B-CUZ YES,,,, U DO)

It is the same as when I recently had a tooth
extracted. "Here we go", I say, loud enough to
be heard this time, as I stomp my way to the
other end of the room.

DEAR LIBROCUBICULARIST, YOU ARE NOW, AT THIS TIME, ADVISED, BY ME TO MAKE YOURSELVES EVEN MORE COMFORTABLE. GRAB SOME NIBBLES, A CUP OF TEA, YOUR FAVORITE BLANKET. PERHAPS A MAGAZINE. RUN TO THE SHOPS, CATCH UP ON YOUR FAVORITE SOAPS? RUN SOME ARRANDS. WE ARE GOING TO BE HERE FOR SOME TIME. (Librocubicularist): One who reads in Bed. "The Dentist slashed the back of my throat with one of the tools", she continued.. I bleed (3) hours after, which brought about fainting. When admitted to EMT, asked if I wanted Morphine. "Certainly not, I am allergic", I stated. The pain had become unbearable. I, in the past, had been led to believe, Morphine to be preserved for the terminally ill, or Cancer. As you have guessed, they proceeded to administered Morphine anyways. Rendering me paralyzed for hours at a time. On my approach of solicitors, I am met with total refusal. No case. Still I suffer side effects. No one cares. "Have you not survived?" I asked. "It is almost as if I am never a real person", she says. I do like, and love myself. Partly. Merely never the fact that I am, too weird, or strange, to fit in with this, so called World. Such behavior usually results in anger towards me. I sat, sitting in a dark room as I began to cry. The time reaching nearly (2) am this side of the Globe, and I am nearly 1/2 Centuries old. This sort of thing has played out in my life for over (4) Decades. Where does it end? Me, completely ALONE. Never one visiting Spirit. Lost, frightening, solemn, or otherwise. God, asking me to hang on. But I have hung on. And if there is good, and there are good things coming my way, I shall most likely incur, what I call, A Just around the Corner Happening. Waiting, patiently to insure that it has all been a huge joke. Been there, done that as well. Thing is. I realize and see everything. EVERYTHING. Boring!!!! Even what others may never see. Trust me. A Lonely World, whilst standing parallel it. I relish Winter. There is nothing more Beautiful than ice falling from the sky. On rainy days, I emerge glorious from confinement. Umbrella-Less. Looking around now, I realize that I am the only one getting wet. Others have no idea what I see, or what they are missing. You Get It Now?. You must understand, the very thing bringing me knees height. Today, I can handle being the only person in the world, but in the back of my mind I am far aware of a breaking point brought about by the tiniest of happenings. A stumped toe and my world has fallen sending me to the halls of smoke filled fume-less backdrafts where I shall stand in the hopes of my Son downwind the contact high of a second hand chokings as the overpowering tree musk guard him from such. But still I worry. I am sat before you, though you may never tell as we blind ourselves, one another, divided by laptops keyboards and tablets. Our hands may never connect for we only love what we love, want what we want, care for our own, never another's. This life is shit and I shall dance on my last day naked and out of doors wearing little more than a silly grin and a Fedora hat. Still, consider on Friday nights, when people are planning to get together, I know my name shan't be called. No date arranged. No one is coming to collect me. No one is going to call. No girlfriends have ever, and will never call, to quire after my evening attire in the hopes our outfits may never clash. "But I am here", I said. I can remember a lot of good times. Times when we laughed, felt good, dined in all corners of the World, fell in Love. Cannot, you recall any of that? "Well, she said. Do you remember, about (3) years ago, I lucked up on a man whom, I believed, worshiped me. "Oh Boy", I thought. She would recall this. Never merely that, he is beautiful (U Know where this is headed, do u not)? Right downhill with the rest of my life. We found ourselves together often. A plus. You are Beautiful, He'd say. One more plus. Never asking a name. Gorgeous, he said, this shall forever be your name. 3rd plus. And while far too lovely for walkies, one may suspect him of harboring hidden wings beneath stylish shirts. A roaring voice suggest he is near. Conversation acquaints we. As I ponder long last behind a lifetime of non- love. The freak is I, she said. Along come one lovely soul such as I. Does he love? Or merely speak in all the correct tones? Never vulgar, never negative, never more shall we stand alone. No more shall I pop into the pubs alone. My meals, consumed solely in solitude, minus good conversation with one other than an empty drop box at my Mobile. Staring at the screen which now houses a photo of Daddy, dress- fully attired at aged (19) on the Day he joined the British Royal Marines.

No longer shall we wonder and fantasize at the seemingly happiness of others. A behavior which caused great pity for my own soul. Disgust with myself?? Never. He is often nearby. I scarcely require leave of home. Till one day, low and behold. After a few months, something changed. I begin to get calls from strange Women, asking me why my number had been found amongst theirs, in his mobile. I observed as he approach another women's vehicle, wearing a pair of opened zip Levi's, and very little else. No shirt. He has a lovely body. When asked, may she be known to me, his replied, she is just some old lady from his past. Known the woman for years, he said, and that she had been a tad bit Off Kilter. Off her face, most times, he added. On speaking with the women myself, she seemed puzzled at his disembark-ment from my front walk, as he left my home. Rumor has it, he had described me as same, when explaining his departure. Plus she appeared far younger than myself, but no one would have guessed. In my age range, though, (5) stone over pounds and obviously no source of income to cover her monthly waxing expenses. Turns out he is a Gigolo. (Gigolo): A young man paid or financially supported by an older woman to be her escort or lover. (WIKIPEDIA). How may such a fiasco take place,,, I PONDER. Me, never placing before him a farthing. He never asked. I have neither compensated nor filled his belly. He, never a request. You are the only woman I love. What a joke as I am once more dropped at a knees height proving myself incapable of love or being as. "He is using you", I told her. While all the while using others. A Gigolo? A dammed lousy one, I might add. "Forgive me Sir(s) Progress, Rest, Excitement, Revelation and Contentment. I have once again failed you", sang a rot filled soul. "This Creep is no mere gigolo, she said., angered yet again at remembrances. The Gigolo stands a proud source. A man of substance, hard work, and charisma. He owns up 2-B. He has a lover, money, never the women. The fool lay dormant, silly boy. Choosing by his own admission, the so- called less attractive female. (NO SUCH THING). Perhaps (1 to 2) stone past a faint upon sight body weight. "YUK", she says. I shouldn't have to look at that. "SHOOOSSH", I say. A common thief. A liar. Not a very good one. Even the thief takes pride in himself, his work. He boast it proudly about his chest remaining sloth. Unseen, unheard. Leaving never a scratch upon loosened combination wheels as he once more spin lucky numbers at a wind's blow. And it is back round to (00) double zed and (1). You may never know he's been. "NO", she says. No, this

Son of a Bitch lies to all and every. Pretends to love a woman. (SIN). Makes good love to her in her own warm clean habitat. Her weekly pay tall sandwich for snag to peer about gaze past loves behind the wheel of her well-wheeled terrain. '' The slouch and his fevering Dick shall find a day apart lasting a lifetime'', she says snarling.

(OFFICIAL DEATH REPORT) A Broken Heart????? Right. Ha, ha and I (laff). Just a faze and I have been here before. I know me better than that. I love for so long. Through the abuse, the harsh words. The others, the youthful thinking. The ignorance. Still I waited. "I know that you no longer fancy me", he said. Assuming by present you have found someone else. And if, I said. I had allowed another to erase your touch from my body, what part of you would I have left to call mine? It has been nearly a year, he stated, as if I have never suffered the time in whole. Night after week upon months needing. My Longing, is the one once acquainted. Now changed to a dark figure in passing. As I wait aimlessly for him to appear at my door. I have lay wait 1/2 Decade to find you, I told him. Now a year without you, I would wait forever for you to find yourself. And now these very words which have cleansed him. Renewing his soul. Bringing him fourth, now back to me. I find us embarrassed, as he shall never leave my side. And as I lay here, in gulped in his arms, sweat, wine stains and a whiff of stale seeds and stems. I find that I do not love him. Now what am I to do? Certainly never Commit Suicide. As my heart has found freedom from Want. (LONELINESS): verb; A complexed, unpleasant emotional response to Isolation, or lack of companionship. Stims from heartbreak, lack of activity. Rated, HIGHLY Deadly. Slightly more so than Obesity. I AM, In my own opinion, more deadly than Aids, The Diagnosis of Cancer, Gunfire and Liposuction. Towards the end, I remember my aggravation upon knowing. "Take the pills" one voice said. "No" said another. Aggravation. Every move worked out for me. Every thought. Every puff of cigar, counted . Never do this, or that will happen. Never move your foot to this side, or this will happen. Never stand in this direction, such things may occur, frightening you. A Paranoid. She finds more often than not, paralyzed in fear of what may happen. Fear kept me from living. If I do swallow them, with my luck, (4) minutes after, The World would come a knock, knock, knocking, at my door.

We bring news of great change. Hurray, it would shout. Arise, you Cow of a woman. This has all been a game. You may have Love, friends, Happiness, Cleanliness. Your Children are here. They have come for you. Come, take choice your fancy. Take it, it is yours. By the way, you are Heir to a Dynasty. Take your Throne and these Princely Robes. You are greatly Loved by all. We were wrong in treating you this way. You rightfully so warrant respect. And food. All this, spoken to my lifeless, tear stained, pulse-less body. As it stiffens in shape towards a box of my favorite color lined in my second favorite. No expense spared, for the World is mine, and always has been. Here, all the while. Stuffed between a mattress and a will to Die as I perch, with little to engage myself in gorgeous weather and no lift to arrival. Hidden from the World and shall remain as such. Hungry for a breath of fresh air and the occasional passersby. And now as the rooms in which I once held in sole attendance hover with the Ghost of what should have been my own, alas, in full knowledge of my, (never getting one thing right), they have sent another.

PLEASE, CONTINUE READING. AS I HAVE ASKED PRIOR, CEESE REACHING FOR SO MUCH OF A STORY LINE. TRY AND LEARN SOMETHING. IF ONLY ONE THING FROM WHAT I AM SAYING.

HERES WHERE IT GETS INTERESTING, OR SLIGHTLY MORE INFORMATIVE. YOU CHOOSE.

Observing a commentary on guns. And if you, as Americans, should arm yourselves. Strap up, or be allowed to. In the instance you may encounter, what you believe to be a terrorists. No, I shan't capitalize this word. First of all, there is no such thing. (terrorist): A made-up word. Would there were such a person, or persons, based on the description and bad rap. Would consider themselves, far too aloof, and in total un-allowance to remain, as it were, spotted. terrorist?????,, Walking about, amongst the people?, Shopping in malls?, Employed at what you call Petrol stations?. "Would there were such things, or people as terrorist, one would most certainly have to hole in title P.M. or a King to ever encounter one", she shouts in laughter. Most likely, during a dream after sniffing far too much

Brandy. The people need never dawn firearms locked, loaded, set to harm the innocent as they go about daily life, gracefully attired in what some may call, unusual or religious garb. The human mind has neither evolved, nor has it been privy to what I relay as; The Ability To Conjugate, Common Knowledge. "It has never, nor will it ever be inhabited by the masses. "A chosen few", she says. A chosen few. ©2015. "Like those who shall actually read this", I should gather. This World is Emendated with made up words and phrases.

Politics

Talking too much

Over Dressed

Humanity

Safety

Health Insurance

Health Care

Truth

Pass Tense

Security

Right and Wrong

Human Rights

Confirmation

On Sale

Monogamy

Celebrity as Stars

Equal Rights for Women: Equal rights are fine,
had the word equal meant anything. As a
woman, I agree entirely. NEVER that we may
hold in any attempted truth, the ability to carry
out life changing positions. Politics, which in
its own self is a Great Fallacy. Judge and Jury.
We as Women hold far too much emotion. Far
too little caring, had we missed a shoe sale,
being that it is praying heavily on our minds.
(EXAMPLE): Today I am Judge; OFF WITH
THEIR HEADS. I have yet to enjoy my
morning tea.,, Or better still, I have had my
morning tea. Would have enjoyed it far more
with a teaspoon of that gorgeous brown Raw
Sugar, Case Dismissed, I MUST get myself to
Tea Valia before they are shut.

African American (No such Person)

Pain

Dying

Gone

Old

Talking to Yourself

Faithful

This Price Has Been Reduced

ENTERTAINMENT

Lowest Price Ever

Free WIFI

Clean

Germ Free

Weight Loss Pills

Weight Loss Plan

Best

Better

An Education

Student Loans

Free Will

Alone

Sanitized

Credit Protection

Identity Protection

All Natural

100%

You'll Be Fine

Peace

Enough

Free

Certainty

Trust

Best Friend

It is against the law, or should well be. PLUS
immoral, down to the moment wrong, To Put
Your Hands On Any Woman. One of which
you know, much less, one of which you never

shall, (MEN). This MUST be a made- up phrase. It has been my knowledge most men have never heard of, nor do they appear to comprehend. (Needed to be pointed out)

terrorist

World leaders

Happiness

Royalty

Genuine

Heaven and H@ll (a h@ll) No One Such Place, yet many of, meaning many different forms of.

Real

Cursed

Yahoo Mail

No

Can't

Fastest

Original

Secret

Safe

Not

A Copy Of

Dead

Ugly

Civil Rights

Fat

Awake

Early

Who Cares

Was

New

No One Cares

Legal

INNOCENT UNTIL PROVEN GUILTY (That's a big one)

You Only Live Once. LOL,,,,Really? Wish I'd known sooner, then you would never be here wasting time reading all of this.

And the DOOZIE of them all: ----DOES NOT
EXIST---- (NEVER REPEAT THIS PHRASE). A
Great Risk, my typing such a phrase. Perhaps if
I had written EX***.

Oh well it's far too late now.

ETC.......

One man cannot, (MAY NEVER), lead a
World. The most he can do is represent those
who believe to hold the whole of a World in a
Complete Stupor. ©2015

"Get up". "NOW", I say to her. Set straightened
thy knees, yet releasing buttocks from seat
clinging. Shower. Adorn clean clothes, tame
the main, draw on some lippy. Go outside,
minus the cigar case. Breathe. Get out of this
place. You may never seek, nor find, what you
believe, as a person, this Illusion called
Happiness. We merely come close in this
World. The human mind would explode at the
first step in the right direction of what
Happiness in tales. We are far too gone with
the fact it lies with material goods, full bellies,
and empty ball sacks. Do you dislike me so,
that you would subject my very being to this

lower state of consciences? On the miss-truth that I, who have known you before your time, would allow you to be unhappy had I known we would end up in such a place? The dislike of one's self, may well fall under Sins. (SIN): noun; An Immoral act considered to be Transgression against Devine Law. Sin. One definition of Sin, is doing what is wrong or not doing what is right, according to GOD'S Rule (1 john 3:4). "(Impossible to disobey GOD)". Sin, like Freewill, Too, is an Illusion. Sins, (Fear, Power, Self-Deprecation?). We the Self Deprecators. "We are often seen, heard. Belittling ourselves", she said. All the while think, we, better, wiser, cleaner, more well fed. We look better in our clothing. A most heinous act of Fear and Greed. A feeling I, the better. I, the chosen. I, who (hast) come-eth, yes COMM-ETH.... (The reason for Self-Publish, Self-Binding, and Self Distribution. Had this Book been Edited you would have learned NOTHING). We Descend from other places or afar. And why Fear those such as myself. Apart from being a terrible Mother, A terrible Person, A Terrible Human Being, or sooner Facsimile thereof. (FEAR): An emotion induced by a threat? Alarm? A painful emotion experienced when one is threatened by Danger or EVIL? The origin of FEAR, first known use, before the 12th Century. (Middle English) feren. Old English. The quickest way to get a life is to go for a ride, someone once told me. I cannot at this point recall to whom and when it were. Merely that it occurred somewhere shortly before Alexander Zonjic announced the fact that women cannot apply Mascara with their mouths closed. (ALEXANDER ZONJIC): Born April 30, 1951. A Professional Flutist, from Windsor Ontario. (WIKIPEDIA). I may be a Genius and a Scholar, but I am no Profit, she said proudly (THEN YOU, THE READER, ASK, "WHO ARE YOU? WHO IS THIS?, WHO WROTE THIS?".) HA HA HAAA, she laughs concurringly, as My fingers tire from a journey of hunt and peck and wonder of why the Blooming Heck we need a (G) and an (H) in the middle of every BLOODY word in this English Language ending in (O) sound. Now she, with her yet, un- cut mouth, dropped to the bottom where there is nothing left but hope and Prayer. A place to start each morning. Less our illusion of Free Will allows us to push it to the back of the fridge. Save it for a rainy day, or an old film. Fucks me up. Drives me crazy. A huge waste of time. They may never get it. Not one of them. "They shall belittle it", she cried. Belittle it. As people, we never paid much attention. Never stopped to look around. Smell the roses, as they say. But I have done more than smell the roses. I have taken time to smell the Tortoise. Why do you believe he lives as long as he does? The same reason he moves so slowly. Everything in MODERATION. The Tortoise lives every day in moderation. He walks slowly, eats slowly, probably talks slowly and softly to other Tortoises. Perhaps, even to we. We may never hear him, advising us to slow down. For we are moving far too fast. Aside which, we would never believe the tortoise may well be speaking. Slow down, he says, softly, as we fly past at the speed of light, straight for our demise. The Tortoise, unlike the Hare and Modern Technology, which changes everything. And if you look closely, for the worst. (10) years past I could walk in a beauty shop and for (50) new pennies, acquire (100) bobby pins. One of which, I could obtain the most delicious, better than sex, scratching of my ear. Now for the same £1, I may receive (20) per pack. The edges are rounded now, by use of a far less expensive, lower quality, more un- hard-work -for -the-humans, to obtain or manufacture, Plastic. For some odd reason, to protect a full-grown adult, who has lost the urge and ability to protect themselves from sharp objects now that Modern Science may do it for him. We are losing everything. Even our ability to think for ourselves. The common brain activity. I know, full-on, if I am to stick, a ruff, yes ruff, jagged, sharp edge of any metal object to my ear, I am to proceed with caution. The brain WERE, at one point, all set up to protect me. Evidently, Evolution has replaced these particular Brain wrinkles with a far less expensive plastic by-product of a Human tissue. Replaced by a non-metal bobby pin. Plastic, Plastic. As I dig at my ear to find the same pleasures and await the day when modern technology may shrink an Army of men, armed with metal (or Plastic) garden rakes to climb inside my ears and scrape down the sides. "Cotton bud does the trick", she said. I would never place a white cotton towards my brain. That of which being a form of Voodoo, ... You know not, what you do. Each person is responsible for the next. If I could prove to you that the white cotton towards the center direction of the brain, for example, causes never merely physical harm, but financial loss for a fellow Human Being. One you may never meet. Would you cease to do as such? (Never stick anything White in your ear).

(Superstition: SIN). Trust me. I lack the energy, the words, the patients to place in your minds the understanding of such power. Apart from which they would never publish it in original form. (Self-Published or otherwise). Oh yes, self-published books too, face some scrutiny. There is always a wondering eye. A thieving eye. To instill in you, every word, to make since of such would run a (500) page book and we have very little time left so the information may go amiss. We all possess power. Magic is real. We make magic every day. Some bad, Mostly Bad. Some good. But I tire from the countless calls from the fear- filled literary agents who lack the balls to set truth before well-established publishing houses. "The truth is hidden for a reason", she said. Same reason my credit is in ruin with no explanation. Like someone else could possibly have my same name. My Parents had to be the first Non-White Hippies. Or, more to the point, who is actually WHITE. Caucasian. Paper is white, remember? Were never aware of the Black Youth's ability to obtain good weed in the mid to late 60's (i.e..), my name for fucks sake. They must have been high. Ignorance. For who is really Black. Tar is black. You may be right there. Even I know not everything. With all the education I have had privy to. Daddy, Bless him, lay waste over £1,000,000.00 on my Education.. Still, after all the entered Universities. All I really wanted were an American Standard Fender Stratocaster. Solid Teak wood body, with a Rosewood Fret Board. Pearl Pick Guard and a 24hour, (7) day a week, live -in instructor, to insure I hit an Albert King cognizance of the tongue." Dear Daddy", she said. Daddy has done his very best. You were a stubborn child at the best of times. "He loves you", she said. The pair of them. Daddy, his Money and Social Standing. I have never worked, I have never felt the need to care for myself. And now that I am nearing an end, I have developed this mad dash to do everything I have yet to. Superiority Complex. "You possess (Sup....)". Yea, yea, I know", she said, interrupting me in embarrassment of a cobweb riddled pocketbook, and her own, ever seeming counteracting overworked ego. Daddy, in his sickest of crafts, sickening when he know-eth I inherit (9) times bettering him at his own game. The offspring of Evil, seek- eth restraint. "My Children are free of this curse", she cried. Tis I who ache. Hurting to concur. Though every time my words flow, I have to fucking PISS. Release me gravity, age and

Menopause, for I am busy. I am in no such the mood for her dumb ass today. Gravity, For she is ever present. Tugging Downward my face and nipples. "Nooo", she said, holding her hands to her face, as if to block a blinding light. Never call me, Old Woman. Sit, toying North-Eastward, and await your Angels. I assume she is pertaining to Mother Nature herself, or to her own Mother. If it is her main Beast of Burden, as she refers to the old gal, It is a tad difficult to continue on about the woman at this point, considering we have at (2) minutes prior, shared a laugh. And I, at present, feel no anger towards her at all. But this shall soon change. Actually, I feel quite calm. A frightfully unusual state for one such as myself being who I am and what my mind holds in its (2) broken hearts unable to un-see. I cannot convey to you, if it is my full stomach or the Bogle California 2013 Cabernet, which has caused a great contentment in the day. Can it be the overwhelm-ment of my Birthday outing (3) nights past where I bowled a near perfect game. Were it S.B., looking (10) times his often Best, or the confidence on LXS's face, as he too Bowled Near Flawless. Maybe it were the (2) hour long, shoot the shit, just because, with A.S.R, that has my chest higher than usual.

Were it the Skype from G-Baby, which has me floating in a bubble of belief that the world is an awful place, filled with tiny slices of Euphoria? LOL. No, I shall not, at this point and time, spell out for you, the names of my offspring and loved ones. I have left, in my hole riddled soul, about (1) and 1/2 cups decency. Coupled with, what I measure at perhaps (1) teaspoon of desire to become a Rich Women at the indiscretion of their privacy and safety. But less never I forgive, Mother. Whose name shall also remain un-revealed. (Remember, my love of Contradictions at the beginning)? Mother, were an Evil no small child should encounter. Assuming assumptions. We were often beaten on Mothers assumptions. There is something wrong with all of my Children, she boasted grandly to a crowd, unwilling to remember, yet uncaring at fault. She is the one with the problem. And as for we the offspring lack only in balls bigger than the words to announce to her that you, my dear, were a rotten, terrible Bastard. What mother holds, vail over her child prospering? (No Capitalizations here.) Had you ceased assumption and listened? Had you found there is no problem greater than yourself? I wish to ask. I lay watch as she has lost the sole of her earnings blooming on that same assumption. Or what a tethered mind such as hers had often realized. Festering away behind new and old hairs now lost in luster. Her man her home. All a result of what she herself, hand on heart contest is truly apparent. Then behind truth and reason, insist the highway is her own path, and had better be yours. O Poor, souring beast, stand before me in ruined veins and pain. Never grown past childhood or day of scorn-ment. Now (80) plus (3), shall never grow in mind nor spirit past what one has baked in belief. Sad really. Yet I cannot, nor have I, a longing to save her, as my own sole reaps remorse, restitute, shame. "I should have spoken up for her", she said, regarding her oldest child. My Girl were often exposed to mother's emotional, psychological, and mental torment. I just sat there. Sat, as Mothers words drew her to tears. She were tired is all. She had never hit anyone, much less her younger Brother, and never would. Just another of Mothers assumptions. A day of practice and prejudice, and my poor girl were exhausted. They looked to me, they did. They waited, as gaze upon my mouth bread nothing. Never an utter. No solace, no relief, no Momma, as she laid crying till the overworked

sand men take-eth in haste, my place of
restitution. A nice kip. The all healer is sleep.
Till thy awaken. Opening semi closed and
cracked wounds in half scale with no blood.
And what about the time we sat homeless. "I'm
going to eat she sang twice, with no response
from my fear filled heart, as I wait only for
Mothers acknowledge. "Look at her eating to
make us late", mother stung from her nasty
puss riddled lips. Like a naked spider on his
last fly before his hanging. My poor child
warned us she has yearning, though none of us
listened. Us meaning me and all who sail with
ME." Not you", she said. Now once again, she
looked to me in passed anger. My Oldest, the
strength maker. The poor girl found little
choice. I now find it to have been my very
Daughter who has directed ME, the right turn
on that forked road, Mother hood. You see, I
too, am a rotten, terrible Mother. Terrified of
my own Mother. Horrified at the outcome of
defending my own Children. The hurt I have
conflicted may never seal, she said. My
grandchild, wearing the sweetest of faces may
only mend. "A Time Machine", she shouted. "I
must build a time machine", repeating herself.
Searching about an empty room for materials
to build such, only coming up with nothing

sept empty pop cans and the left over trays where her food is served. Grasping at her torn white dress in hopes of tools and mechanical parts. "I must speak for her and speak loudly ", she cried. Fear. Fear has allowed my Mother 's cruelty to rein over them. The Crazy girl drove walkway bound on lieu of a school gathering and shouting proudly at a car park attendant the fact he were in front of her car. "But you're on the walk", I should have said. My Children have suffered my fears. Never to mention as we approached the gathering I found that all the other Mothers had arrived with treats. Where lay my Contribution?????, I could have at least baked a small cake, or stopped for a box of donuts, I thought, as I looked upon my daughters, Grandmother scorned face. I were a sorry excuse for a mother myself, so why condemn her. Why, I might ask. Raised by fear himself. A time machine indeed.!!! I would probably screw it up worse. But the bad memories never cease. My sorry ass Mother hood renderings. I loved them, so why were I so Bad at it? Why am I so mean? Why am I now that my children have reached their adulthood? Am I no longer that person? My mind displays nothing more than poor memories of late. Bad memories, played out like a movie trailer at the climax of a long awaited reveal of the Murderer set in a 1940's Who Done it. Nasty remembrances. Things I have done. Things, done to me. Things, I have said, but should never have. Things, unable to un-see. The times when I could have accompanied the girls to the Doctors. My child and grandchild. "I have missed out," she cried. Would you like to come with us Mom, she asked. No, I said, No.?... Where were I? What had I to do more important than. And there voices, had never, offended me on that quiet knight when lovers speak as she spoke to hear her husband voice. How wonder-ous it is to hear a lover's voice answering one's own, in the dark. But I have destroyed all of that. "Who were I, and why were you there", she asked, surrounded in a haze of anger and black smoke. You have ruined me and I shall dance at your demised carcass fully digested in the stomachs of Falcons. As you lay to fester upon the rock you hale righteous. The Vultures rarely get this far, you do understand. And when I am senior, I shall hang overpriced Fedoras in a huge loft, slightly to the North of Paris. I shall line (9) stainless steel bowls with heavy cream for 9 felines. Yes, I fancy (9) felines, Persian rugs, and any and everything

Restoration Hardware can squeeze into a (4000) sq. ft. space with 30ft. vaulted ceilings. White hair and a wig of the same for rainy weather. Seeing as my foot still persist to hurt singular. When asked by a physicians and priest, I shall explain how it spat out green, shortly before spinning round (3) times, as if to be possessed. (NOT CAPITALIZING THAT WORD EITHER). I shall smoke (2) Cigars a day, the huge Churchill's, as they replace the vitamins in Beer and Sunshine. I fancy Wine and the Rainy Season as I lay staring at said ceiling in complete reminiscence, the best part being a women, and it would seem you have seen far too many Brit-Coms. In (2) words, (I shall never divulge his name). One of Thee, most beautiful. The man who need be cloned 3.52 billion times, Insuring every women a happy life. Though a public figure, we must never take ownership. Though, he, an actor, the best in my books, we shall never embarrass. I am sure he has a family who loves him. I have never, the right to call upon his name in public humiliation for my own use merely because he starred in many a film, she said. I have never, the right to intrude. He gives me a Genuine Smile. Something I have yet to experience for some time. Something I had forgotten about. Forgotten how good it felt. "That is well enough for me", she said. Without the heart break of (EVERY MAN CHEATS) syndrome. (As of 12/28/2015), There are, said to be 3.52 Billion women inhabiting the Earth); Google search. May we have his initials? "No way", she said, frowning. You would be sure to know. But enuff, "Yes, ENUFF, about men", she said, interrupting me yet again. Merely a celebrity crush, we all have them. Now who is wasting time? "Who cares"?, I shout. Finding a man is like Travel or the choosing of Tender for a new Boat. Get my (Shit) together, then make add-ons. My mind, my piece of mind, my finances to be set straight, my home, mode of transportation. Furniture. House hold needs in place. My health, mental state. My appearance, fill my cupboards, my dressing room. Expenses, paid. Pantry, full with what is needed. My Children, My Grandchildren, tucked, Educated, Fed. Well-Fed. And then, some day, When all is in order and I find myself sitting once more in one spot. This time looking out of many a floor to ceiling, CLEAN, sunlit window. I shall choose a small quaint (52) footer to fill my days with Fresh Sea air. Replacing the loneliness, they have grown so attached. I shall venture out to a near-by watering hole and engage in conversation, someone who, although, never too much like myself. Enough like me to understand. Perhaps I too, shall begin a new relationship. Insuring that my bed, as it is so named, shall no longer feel the cold hand of the one- sided pillow-ness of which it has become so accustomed. Until then, I spawn from the punisher. Yet my hands fade to cotton as I strike. The last known descendant from those with Diamond edged words. Though mine dull between head and heart. A walking dissention from those whose selfless control less no buffers, no fear of repercussion. And now my (10) minutes are ones I hold dear. I wear it proudly about my sleeve. "Are you clean," she asked. In full ear of my Brother. "Yeah,,,, You Have Said ", I reminded She. Placing in plain view, AND SHALL WE NEVER FORGET. Mucky yummies worn by an (11) year old girl. We have been here before. This so amazed my sickened sibling. Only never too amused at torture towards one held perfect in his eyes. Finally, he must has thought. "The witch is dead," his heart sang, as he boasted about the neighboring fellows of how I. I of all have at last been dethroned. A right thrashing, I must say. While he, the all mighty, may well have been beaten numb for merely choosing a wrong tie, in the eyes of Father and company. He remains the victim. He had at an early age warned them of your very coming, but no one would listen. I feel (Sik), I am a (Sik), Sad, Lonely core of deceit and filth. A cave of thoughts, bloody puss filled hurts and un-forgives. I grow cobwebs and maggots upon golden unpolished light capturing Authenticity as it awaits a capture who shall aspire its knowledge, release it from its confinement, polish it well, find its true value, then display it for all to see. For a small fee, of course. We were often beaten for a reason. The only reason being whatever Mother believe in her sour head that we had done, or what she in her sickened mind, decided at a moment's notice, we were thinking, or what she thought a word from our mouths really meant. "WUD U SHT DA FK UP ABT CHO MMA", I, at that very moment would have texted her. But the woman has little need for a mobile. "You misinterpret everything", Father once told her, she continues. As he too, felt a wrath of childhood hindering's at the hand of The Madmen with the foot of a Crow, gripping (3) broken, bloodied, poison arrows." I am sik, Yes, SIK", she said. Sick minus the (c). I am sik and they may all see it. Neutrals and Normalcies. I should entitle this Book 'Neutrals and Normalcies'. "You could well name it Daddy. It is never too late", I said. Or better still, MAD COW DESEASE. We all long for what we cannot have. May never possess. I have said it time and again, on disbelief something so simple seems so far from light. Perhaps (ICEBREAKER), seeing as how well I enjoyed writing it. Far better than this Buggery. "Perhaps even grow my own food". A doorway leading me out, then back in. A doorway unseen, unheard by lower middle class conversation with envying eyes. But I do not need this, Mother would say. Words never lay-ed upon ears of my own Offspring. Is why they prosper then smile back at me upon departure into the world, looking both ways, with 1-1= Decidophobic tendencies. (Decidophobic): DECIDOPHOBIA; Fear of Making Decisions. And I remember now, their killing of me. Parental Units. The Promise- Un- Keepers. My demented Mother. Jerking me around, as I explained, I am unable to move for fear of heart failure. But in her sickened mind, believes illness to be a competition. And only one of we were to have an illness at a time.

Following her operation, no one else were allowed to become ill nor complain of anything short of overeating. While even at deaths door, we surrendered stomach gas for fear of crucifixion. I were far too ill to move that day. The look upon my face angered this diseased creature, as I lay cross- legged on a self- souled shagged carpeted floor trying to keep a straight face. Dying, bleeding. In an ill attempt to hide my pain, allowed everyone to leave. Leave me there with the beast instead of demanding help. A power I have gained all too late. And might I quote;,, "Get up from there", she shouted. U just hurtin cuz i'm hurtin. End Quote.. So I had to move. Bleeding more now. Unable to breath, as my lungs fill with more oxygen than needed. A time Machine I always said, A time Machine, and I shall return. Slaughtering the beast. Beheading her. Placing her ugly topper upon a very tall poll towards the sun. As it rots further in the heat of destiny, before being eaten by the very crows she fester from thy crack-ed mouth. "Then, and only then, shall I stand unafraid", she said. "And you shall stand close by?",,, she asked. May neither the height of tall stick nor the stench of tormented flesh, send me on this day. I shall stand fast like worried warriors in heed of

Karma's warning. Then I shall take thy Punishment, wearing it proudly about my fedora for all who sail in her. (I use the term often. I like it, and so you shall now use it. Fit it into your next conversation and watch as eyes widen). "The clock reads (6) minutes to (6) and I have not had sex in (6) months", she said, rolling about the floor like a cat in heat. "Can't help you with that one", I said, shaking my head, but in no disbelief, if you have read any of the preceding. I find it hard to believe that you shall meet anyone sitting on your ass. Apart from which, have never we left it a bit late for the (3) sixes phenomenon? Open Toe,, you are not getting any younger. "Age is but a myth", she said, righting herself. "I can tell the way a man shakes a Martini if he is well hard to please", she said. " Or Homosexual", might I add. The way a women stands, drives and forms her words, if or not, she has an abusive spouse.

A WOMENS HAIR DENOTES HER INTELEGENCE.
YOU COULD EASILY HAVE PLACED A FEW
ROLLERS IN THE NIGHT BEFORE AND CAPTURED
THE RESPECT OF ALL STANDING. SOONER THAN
THAT, (I JUST RELASED A WET TOWEL IN RUBBING
MOTION WITH NO BUMPED ENDS) WHEN YOU
KNEW THE CAMERAS WOULD BE THERE AT FIRST
LIGHT, SILLY GIRL. AN EVEN MORE ACUTE EYE
DETECTS WEATHER YOU AR FULLY, PRE OR POST
MENSTRIAL, BY THE DAYS CHOICE OF CLOTHING
AND ACCESSORIES. COME NOW. PURPLE TIGHTS
AND YELLOW RUBBER WELLIES, WHO ARE WE
FOOLING?

The way a person wears a tie, or hat weather or
not he or she is a liar, a cheat. The cut of ones
fingernails determines whether they are Pale or
Dark Horsed. Though I am no Sherlock
Holmes. Or sooner, that he were no me. Like
other extraordinaire, we were a long time
coming. Our stories twisted. If you have no
recollection of Sherlock Holmes, you are far too
young to read this. Please return my book to
your Parents Library. Immediately. Today is
1/8/16, last night I experienced thee most odd
of dreams staring none other than Living
Legend, Clint Eastwood Himself. He destroyed
the powder room after a long chat with old
figures from a 1940's western outside on my
old sunporch sat next to a set of antique chest
spray painted white. "Hi", he said, directly into

my face and close enough to feel the breath
from old gun slinging films. Which I, as a
child, found to be a tab bit boring. Once again,
I say, RUDE. You know nothing of the Man.
On his descent, as I listened at the door to here
one of the worlds sexiest men to wash from his
boots, dirt and mud. Splattered to the walls.
While I, in hopes of a quickie with a (93) year
old living legend in my childhood home. "How
are you", I say. To no surprise of the
humbleness of one so high in stature. The man
has just splattered old western boot mud about
the walls of my Powder room. Normally, I will
have a particular dream of a particular
someone, forget, then (3) days later learn of
their Death. Almost as if they were contacting
me for guidance. But this time nothing, and I
am overjoyed. Clint is still going strong and
may he reach the (100) mark in good health.
"There is little difference in life and death, sept
we have no longer use for physical body", she
said. Your body may let you down, but you
shall forever remain in good health. If the
living may open their eyes, as I have during
my life. They may see and hear us. Agreeing,
laughing at their jokes. Catching them before
they fall. Finding lost things, re-placing them
in the spot where you have just looked. A

friend of my youngest placed before him a
photo. But asked him to clinch his buttocks. It
were an image of me. Peering from an enclosed
glass walk across which connect one building
to another. The location astonished me.
Though my Son had no recollection of its
meaning or when my image may have been
captured. Immediately, I knew. I KNEW. I
would often find myself at this very location in
Prayer. No matter where I actually place
footage in the World. My mind took me to this
very location. As he looked upon the photo,
my face began to fade as he begins to weep.
This is where I am as I pray, I thought. The
photo, dated well after my Death. I lack recall
of many occurrences following my Death. It
were either there or our front perch. One of the
few places visited during Prayer in progress.
We all go somewhere. Visualize a certain place
during deep Prayer. (Tho), yes,,,, THO, I
fancied visiting the bell tower of that church
overlooking our Loft in St. Germaine. "The
moment of my passing", I said. I shall wait for
them there." I often do", she said. I often wait,
as I stare at the sky. Looking into your eyes.
Your, meaning everyone in the world. My lone
wish is that you may hear, feel the pain I
encumber. How alone I am. Begging for help. I

am pitiful. Is there any help healing warmth? "A hug?", she said. No one, apart from myself is willing to give more than. So I must leave you. You, meaning the world. I love you, all the while needing you to hear me. Hence, this Book. I want to go before my offspring and theirs. Remember my wish. No time machine, as my view of you water over the clouds, dark leaving too soon. I would like to stay but must go before they. I shall never burry them. I shall sooner take my own Life or Death. The two, I now find, being one in the same. If they need an escape, had I been better able to express life, I may be surrounded by many. I had to go. What no one seems to realize is that I were completely sad and alone. After-all, who could bring themselves to Love one such as myself. Be strong enough. I had alienated myself from any activities I may have been involved in. There were Birthday Dinners, Graduations. Celebrations. All of my old hanging buddies, on with their lives. As I sit rusted to the same spot as when we first met. No one to be had in my favorite food joints. No rescue. Nothing to eat when money were at a not. No road trips about the US. No Hikes through Europe, as I sat alone with nowhere else to go. No one looking for me to show up and unhappy with

my location. Full grown now. No small
Children to look after. No deadlines. No job.
Certainly no friends and most of all needing a
change of scenery. No one to ask. Just the await
of the call, shouting (Pack Your Bag), that
never came and never shall. Still I would sit.
When call did arise, it sang, So To Geneva, to
burry my Dear Father. What a lovely, Horrible
journey, as I seem hesitant to glance from a
small window of a small, lonely, greedy
Family owned plane accompanied by nothing
more than the same family with the same
damn conversations ringing my ears that I
have grown ever so tired of hearing while
these tears which blind me now that Daddy
has gone and I sit a dirty ass here in thy very
plane Daddy once dawned for work and play.
"I feel quite numb," she says. A tad bit Stupid,
actually. I have always been made to feel
different. Non-fit, is never, ignorant, or slow.
My father once scolded me " You, my child, are
quite,,, Stupid," he said in worrying voices.
"You've a bloody cheek", my hasted response.
A response to this very day, I hold in great
disbelief of the fleeing from these lips, as you
were never to contradict Daddy. Insisting he
were right, I felt as if he were. It remains such a
shock. A blast of hurt to the heart to hear. I

would never say such to my own. Never on shock of notice-ment, my traits in them. I shall play along. Changing it up as always. Insuring each word spoken, or realization, the most important part of the day. I found myself often hurt by a look or tantrum. My fault, as I infuriate others. Regardless of the relation.... " I have it", I shout, as I leap from my confined space. "A new title for this BOOK", I say,,, SELF PITTY. "But I would never let on", she said, continuing on with the self-pity as if I have said nothing. The hurt, never brought about by my offspring, as Mother would have been. We were often sat, afraid. Downhearted. Ashamed by her words of which we have hurt her or made her feel bad or unloved. How disgusting. We were taught that we made poor Mother feel bad. We were led to believe we caused everyone feel bad. Our own faults. There-fore we never fought back. Even when bullied it remain our fault. We make others feel bad. I am old enough now to know, if you teach a Child to be stupid he grows up to be stupid and there is no known cure, trust me. Here I sit. Alone, again. Closer to (4) and six than the number (10). Crying alone. Hungry, in the dark. Though my android says 3:50pm. Never in my native Scandinavian. It remains dark for weeks on end there. It has always remained dark in my lair. "We could always title the book, (Mommy Issues)", I said, looking up from the Lenovo. "Or (Name Dropper's Anonymous)", she replied, as my smile fade into nothing-ness. I cry so often that there is no longer room for cosmetics upon the eye. One may never capture the hue for the swelling, so why bother. "No", she said. I must retreat. I had to be sure he were secure before I am off to see the World once more, for the final time, I fear. Excited, sept for the fact I shall be alone. I shall move about unseen once more. I have been alone for life. This one anyway. I shall be alone now. Once again, seeing others. Seeing what others may never. Aware of each thought, as my cornered eye lock catch-eth what they take for granite. I shall neither laugh nor cheer, because no one will respond. I shall not clap, because no one is performing for me. Why should they. After all, it is for the others. Never for me. If the audiences were full of those such as myself, the actors would merely postpone all shows. You reek of depression remarked White Cake, following a You Tube comment I once made concerning an EastEnders episode. Is it that obvious? My reply. Bringing all who read it to laughter.

Thinking me to be wise and un-scave-ed, had no idea. But I like White Cake. Shall you forever remain in full able-ment, the ability to take a (4) word sentence to sum up my life, though we have never met... My sort of human Being... Often leaving smiles on my doorstep. Leaving depression behind the humor. Humor behind the depression.

Playing an idiot is well and fine during ones childhood. I had earlier on excepted the fact that this is what life is all about. Even then, I consider it to be quite unfair. As I grew older, I witnessed other people's lives and I realized. I had been given the short end. (NEVER). Angered at the hand I had been dealt. I found the majority of my time on a mad hunt for answers and comparisons. Answers. Questions. Or more so, the balls to ask these questions. There (is) happiness out there and I wanted a piece of it. It all became clear during a lunch at our American school. Somewhere around grade (6). I had been spanked yesterday, said a male classmate. What about the day before? I proceed to ask. Nope, his hasty reply. What about the day before that? I asked in confusion. Nope, his reply. Tomorrow? I naïvely ask. He has now given me the very look I am often given. (What A

Dummy), is the look. I use to dread handing in my papers, Job applications. Anything with my name on filled by me. The reaction remain consistent. And I learned to time it. Always the same. (4) seconds before the forehead would collapse to a mass of wrinkled confusion. I had sense or since stopped handing in papers and filling out forms. We get hit every day, I now realize, but felt far past ashamed to say. I then began to realize that something were wrong. Especially after he replied,, I lay peculiar display of a disturbing behavior this morning and I shall not tomorrow. OH, NO, I thought to myself, with my heart beating out of control. I had not displayed a disarming behavior prior to my spankings. Surely nothing that I had been aware of. And certainly nothing on purpose. On any day. Nor had I planned on it. I then found that I may have discovered a pattern on our beatings. Had mother believed we were thinking something, well,,, I mean, that were that. The woman would often misinterpret everything. This, I found to be extremely un-fair. Un-Safe. I began to h@te her. Still I harbor loathing towards the woman.. Never, may one forget. Never ask me to forgive. It were never fair and I wanted out. As I continue struggle on such a path, I am afraid to visit museums. Afraid of anything which towers more than (1) or (2) feet above my head. My Megalo-phobic state binds me in place, expanding greatly like a pound of Gorilla glue immersed in a (10) liter bucket of water. Expanding till there may be no air left for me. Locking me in place. "I may neither move, nor scream", she said. (MEGALOPHOBIA) Megalo: Greek, Large. Fear of large objects. (Repetition, I may latter test you on these) LOL. I fear entry upon Large White Marbled rooms. I feel cramped, as if I were taking up the last bit of stretching room, or air housed by giants. Hidden from the world. Until set cure shrink-eth them. Washing away all knowledge of their size and strength. The Saatchi Collection? Is that the one with the Shark Frozen in Formaldehyde? I am never sure I have spelled it correctly. Or that I may or may not have mentioned the correct Artist. PLEASE, feel free to send me an Email and we shall discuss it. A big NO, if you are expecting me to view any of the prior mentioned exhibits in person. LOL Anything captured, locked in a lifelike state, larger than life or in real size, may shatter my heart times (3). Causing me to pee blood in plain view of you. Soiling my pants with no spare. Ruining my day and the outing for all who accompany me. (NECROPHOBIA): Fear of dead things. (SOCIOPHOBIA): Fear of Social Situations. Better still, please drop me a Post. As people, we never more connect and emails disturb me greatly. I, at present possess the real number of 8,000,000 plus, so I may never get around to actually reading it, but would love to: P.O. box 402 Royal Oak, MI. 48068 (USA)

RIGHT,,,, (PAUSE)...

Dear Computer, I am neither Profit nor Angel. If my tiny, wee brain allows me to decide I should, at a time, hit save, PLEASE SAVE. I am but a mere Writer. I luck up on Remembrance. I too, luck up on where to put what where. I do not, nor have I, nor will I, Luck Up on Greatness again (EVER). This is a one of. So for the sake of this poor feeble, whining child,,,, IF I ASK YOU TO SAVE,,,, SSSAAAVVVEE. I find it Bloody tiresome as it is, the translation to English. As I have been quoted Deadline for such Literature. Both by numerous publication houses, as well as the e-noc-tour-ous She. She, who lay most impatient, as I peck away sore fingers and carpal tunnels in time to remember what has been spewed by our esteemed hostess. And if you may Pardon the expression, Pig Latin: A language game in which words in English are altered. The objective is to conceal the meaning of the words from others never familiar with the rules. The reference to Latin is a deliberate misnomer, as it is simply, a form of jargon, used only for its English connotations as a strange and foreign-sounding language. (Wikipedia, The free Encyclopedia). Latin: Latin is a classical language belonging to the Italic branch of the Indo-European languages. The Latin alphabet is derived from the Etruscan and Greek alphabets. Latin, originally spoken in Latium, Italy. Through the power of the Roman Republic, it became the dominant language, initially in Italy and subsequently throughout the Roman Empire. (Wikipedia, The free Encyclopedia). Neither of which to be confused with THE LANGUAGE OF THE CURSED. Un like the Curse of speaking English: Countries who share English as a dominant Language also share many other unfortunate attributes, such as self-control, as written by Clive Hamilton. She speaks All Language of the cursed, as I speak a mere (9) languages. I hail Scandinavian. Speaking, German, French, Svenska, along with many others. English is my 9th Language. The last of which I may need speak, or speak of. English, being the Hardest. It has taken we, yes we, a fort night to translate a single page so that you, our esteemed English speaker, may incur a small glimpse of what her life in tales. Compared to when a friend of my daughters explained how a friend of hers witnessed an, unfortunately, never an un-rare and certainly unseeingly, disgusting display of personal space destroying act upon the rights of women. Afterwards walked straight passed, the girl lived to witness him, saying, (And as I walked passed he gave me an evil look). After given statement, she were able to ask the man, why did you not attack me. His reply, because you had those (2) Big Black guys with you. The fact that the girl had been alone at the time terrified her. The fact that he would abuse such a beautiful gift in exchange for abusing women terrifies me. "Same as the Harry potter project", she said. This guy obviously chose Slithering. She often leads me on in order to teach me something. "Keep writing", she said. The common reader never knows what he has read until he has read it. Even if he reads it over and over. He may get it, he may never. "OK, Time". I say to you, The Reader. Forming my hands into a capital (T). Time out. Stop, Put the book down. Dear (COMMON) Reader, Do you mind settling an argument for us? "What are you doing", she asked. "I require immediate feedback," I said. Email me now, My (Never So Common) Reader. Though I prefer a hand- written post, if possible. Feedback. Do you not know what you are reading until you have read it?

Comments now being read, at: MYEXTRAORDINARY9FEARSOFMONUME NTS@ROCKETMAIL.COM along with the post box given above.

Subject Matter: BOOK - P

Thank You.

Fill in here.

_____

_____

_____

_____

_____

_____

_____

_____

_____

_____

_____

_____

_____

_____

_____

_____

_____

_____

_____

_____

_____

_____

_____

_____

_____

_____

_____

_____.

Right, send me a copy of your own input. I would love to read it. Thank You.

'Stop wasting time," she said. "I have few days left", she contest to me. She, who is left in silence. She, who speaks many languages, but never speaks,. Perhaps it is she who has attached this stigmata to my good name. What is this Dictionary fasciation of yours? This constant need to define anything you believe in that tiny mind of yours that the Reader may never understand. "I am no show off," she says, as her back is now to me. My intent is to educate my Reader. Never to display my vast knowledge of a world so unworthy of my presents. "While you are at it", why not ask if we need include, in laymen's terms.", she said. Not everyone is beneath you," I said. "Write Bitch, write", she yells in a frantic frenzy of dirty, tattered hair. You have but (23,065) words, a novel requires (80,000) plus, and NO ONE shall ever publish the short fiction. I thought we were self-publishing. So here I sit, sat, sitting, in hopes to pull from my ass and hers, another (60,000) plus, puss filled remembrances of a life, I, on my own, have

chosen to forget but cannot. (THAT
SENTENCE SHOULD HAVE BEEN READ
WITH THE HEAVIEST COCKNY YOU
COULD MUSTER). Most of the time, I remain
here on my own. Waiting with little to comfort
me sept for a lone leaf warbler perched on the
window ceil as we together await your arrival.
I once encountered her at Cambridge. A
Willow Warbler. I would teach Greek
Mythology to the locals, and Expats alike.
Now, here I sit, listening to you. "Well,,,, come
on", I said. Spit it out. I have already told you
everything, she said. "Then we shall start from
the beginning", I said. Right, but if I repeat
myself, TUFF. If I contradict myself,
AWESOME. If I practice what I preach, please
forgive me. By the way, I count (24,560) words.
"I have had the advantage of speaking English
for (3) plus decades now", she said. "Well I
have not", I said. And good on me. I fancy the
occasional outing. Can you possibly imagine
the hurt of an itch? An itch which indicate,
now changing subject mid- convo, as I like to
call it. The scene is Friday night, get dolled up
go to that Pub down on Campus where there is
always a line to get indoors. And in that line
are some of the most Interesting looking
people. People who attire themselves similar

and probably share the same interest. Then right after you Lay flat the perfect get up, choose the right shoes, You recall to a left sided brain cell, it will all be for nothing, because you, You My Dear, may never belong with Other People. You immediately right your stance. Uninflated your happy chest. Affix the bedroom door, sit on the bed, tuck your head firmly into your stomach in hopes you have cried yourself soundly prior to your offspring's arrival home. You do not need friends, mother would say., And how I do, ever so often tire from remembering. Discussing the mere thought of her. I wanted to be happy. Her problems are not mine. I am not my mother. Then again I sicken to my stomach, PEOPLE watching. The smiling. Greeting friends. Laughing, enjoying themselves. Something, as a Person, I may never experience. To cap it off, they arrived in auto. They shall drive home in cars. HOME, meaning an apartment rented, credit approved. A common result of they work the day away. Which means they have ability to sit at a desk in a Berber floored room filled with (in-adequate) sun acquainting windows. They get along with OTHER PEOPLE. I find that I am in no real mood to conjugate my differentials. Nor am I in such a

mood for remembrances' of. When I require a
night out, A long dark car shall appear. I shall
remain unacquainted with the driver. Knowing
him never from Adam, conversation is Nil. I
shall appear at the door of the pub. And once I
have concluded my resentment of the natives,
the car and driver shall re-appear outside of
that watering hole. I shall mount my steed and
off. ALONE. Then it is back to this cold cell I
call home to await yet another lesson on how I
differ from the rest. "So, I shall stay put", she
said. I shall remain here until my time is done.
Never again shall I emerge from the safety of
shelter-ed-ness, in an ill attempt to wrong
prove my Angels who have worked tireless,
night and day on the improvement of my craft.
Every soul on my bloodline has suffered abuse
from this society. Why am I the only one with
the likes of you?. Perhaps you are the Favor -
rite, or maybe you have simply suffered more
than the others. More than you realize.
"Impossible", I said. Ask mother, she said.
She'll be more than happy to remind you of
who and what you are. On gather, if I am, or
were a favorite, how in heavens name are my
siblings to stand bold as brass, sure, smiling.
Yet never letting on. In one peace? Elmer's
would profit a fortune. "You cannot see the

seams at all", she said, prancing proudly about this filthy room, one hand about her hip, the other pointing downward, in a drunken teapot sort of stance. "(29,340) words", I said. Owing to the fact that the first (29,000) have sparked the interest of no one, and the (340) came from me, I would say we get to work, and fast. We must write, you see. This is all we have. Friday night, all the normal people have dates. We are the ones sat here with nothing. We had well make use of our time. "Come on", she says, fanning me her way as she kneeled towards an East facing wall. The time now reads 8pm. Let us say our Prayers", she said, proudly. Then we shall go out on the lawn and smoke a cigar. David Bowie has passed. I must seek relief from my depression. I miss him. I have always loved him. Jump, they say, JUMP. My favorite Bowie tune. I love Bowie. " How very Rude", I say. To mention one's name sooner or no he remain a public figure. "Someone whom you have never before met", I say. As we have just come to the realization of losing Mr. Rumbold. (Nicholas Smith): Nicholas John Smith were an English actor. He is best known for his role in the BBC sitcom Are You Being Served?, in which he played Mr. Rumbold, the manager of the fictional Grace Brothers department store.

If you have no known knowledge of David Bowie, who he is, I prefer you never to reading my Book. (Joke). It has been rumored that President Jimmy Carter, One of my all-time Favorite American Politicians, has been stricken with Cancer. (Today is 1/15/2016). And never I bare the heart to ever watch Since or Sence and Sensibility ever again. "All of my old Heroes are gone", she said, looking up at the night sky. "They have not left you", I said, snuffing out my cigar with my tongue. A most dangerous, disapproved of, but an O, ever so delicious habit. I too may wind down a cancerous clock. "If they cut off your lips you may no longer wear that overpriced lippy", she said. Then you shall die of heart break. Heartbreak for yourself, longing to stare once more at that doll face you call youth. Then here I shall sit, awaiting my slumber for a mere glance at you, as you, like the others interrupt my dreams of love with one of my most beloved actors, as he stands before me, wearing nothing more than a pair of fully unzipped white trousers, and no (Y) fronts. "He is your daughter's age", I say to her laughing. "He is a Man", she snaps. A Lovely one, I might add. . I thought you loved Ry......"BLOODY HECK", I said, exposing my gritted teeth. Sorry. Nearly released the Blue Canary. The world is round, she said, and Love raps round it uncountable times daily. Never to mention, Sir E. F. gets better looking by the minute. "Sir?", I say, in confusion. Knighted?,.,. Has he been Knighted?, "I'll do it". Her Majesty must have forgotten, she said. He and that poor Obama fellows have been waiting for hours. Never, I recall one Black Man holds the title, or am I mistaken? Clearly an oversight, I can assure you. "You hold in a high BITCH attitude today. Keep this up and you may very well give a cheery wave bye-bye to Harper-Collins". (Harper-Collins): **Publishers LLC** is one of the world's largest publishing companies and is part of the "Big Five" English-language publishing companies, alongside, Hachette Holtzbrinck / Macmillan, Penguin Random House and Simon and Schuster.

"Yea, yea", she said, fanning me away. "Turn around", she slurs. I must spend a penny. Now, where is that beaker? "Steady On", I say, staggering backwards. You splattered the power brick. One more squirt and I shall find myself writing this shit by hand. As you bitch and moan about having no friends and your inability to afford a new laptop. "You dead rarely annoy me during my Period. Only slightly less than the living, she said. You, much like the living, never say what you truly mean. Never telling me exactly what it is you actually want from me. "What Do You Want from me"?, she shouted. WHAT IS THIS THING WHICH YOU REQUIRE? I cannot help you, I cannot help myself. I have nothing to offer. Some reach for me with hands of black smoke dissipating as I reach to console them. I search hard to resist, though at times seems impossible. I cannot go, I say. I shall remain un- ready. I expect a package from Amazon.com any day now. I cannot die right now. (Amazon): Dude, if you don't know, well. "Come on man", I say, in all impatiens to get somewhere else other than here. (36,600) words. (50,000) to go. Your Math's are better than mine, she said. Well, I said. You surely never want to quit right at (80,000) do you? Play the game. I retire defeated. All this reminds me of that dream I had about (KC),. "You remember", she said. I have told you. Your friend, the same? Assassinated over (2) decades ago? "Spot on", she said, shaking her head and turning away. I often dream of her. In a recent dream, she asked if I would accompany her to the 7th floor of a large shopping gallery. With shopping bags in hand, I remain few of the ones who require food. She waited a time for me before being asked to move on. Are you leaving me? I asked. I am not leaving you, she said, I am merely leaving. She then proceeded walked on, out of the food shop, pick up her bags, slowly walking towards the elevators wearing nothing more than a small teal T- shirt, a tiny pair of Pale pink shorty shorts and flip flops. A far cry from her former post Death attire. An old dirty Mack, a dirty face and a frown. As she would often stand, angered in a dirty compound surrounded by flattened un-recyclable automobiles. She often comes for me and is always whisked away. Warned to leave me where I am. Demanded to show me the way back. So they do not leave you, they just leave. Or so you believe. "Let us go in", she said. I cannot bare the sight of bird shit. Upon, our return, she starts right in. " Ok", she said. Let us see, oh yea, (You Don't need): Mothers favorite phrase. (AND,,,,,,, Here we are again), I figure. As I roll my eyes to the ceiling. Never say things such as this to your children then sit pray crying asking what is wrong with them. "O how I tire of she" she said. I want to speak my mind. O how I tire of saying what I think they want to hear just to find they either believe me to be a fool or it's just never what

they wish to hear. I so tire of changing my
words to hide their feelings. ''Fuk' em'', I am
an adult, or so I suppose. What must I fear? I
need another smoke. "I want an end to this",
she said. My head shall swell then explode
upon release of yet another smiling success
story past thy eyes. I, the daily reminder of
how a life, so precious, may dissipate through
cracks of nothingness like a vaporized fume or
overworked kettle. Leaving tattered, destitute,
yearning to set or be set free. "I, a grown up in
spirit", she once sang soundly.
(Atomosophobia): Fear of atomic explosions.
Her eyes water-fall-ed, standing in a crystal
clean snow white room with never a speck of
dirt and every (acugement),??, what's the word
for luxury nick knacks, and bits and bobs? A
women could desire. But I too have seen them.
Had I a Head full of brains, a Bank full of
Pounds, I too may have worn a smile full of
adventure seeking teeth. I too may have
packed a back filled rock climbing lesson-less
free filled Weekends. Had I too placed A home
in Bam-booed black beneath thy feet to a wall
of egg-shelled paint with front-loaded clean
smelling attire in mudded room were my (4)
year old Liver and White Springer Spaniel
shakes day-old traction from his well-

manicured fur. I am a Dog Lover. I too may have worn smiles of the unknowers. ''We grew up with German Ridge-Backs, you know''. Winston and Newton they were called. "Winston were the girl", she said proudly with an over privileged grin. "Not surprising", I said. Your British Short hair, also female, and you named her Leroy. "Thou hast ruined me", she said. All which remains is desire. I were half passed (30) before my legs crossed doors of already body laced chairs, in heed their lessons. They will not like you, Mother said, You are not like them. Stay here, she said. I recall a small gathering of girls in aged, my own feather. Same as workplace. Perhaps they may never desire my company. I am never like them so I stay here. A Lame. Or perhaps I lost my bottle on that last one. They have betrayed me. "They have let me down", she said. As I lay longing for their Deaths, I leave them to wonder aimless in their old age without me. Without my Forgiveness. I forget nothing, and have forgiven even less. (Believe in All Practice few)©2010. But they shall never hear as my words pass through many Auditory passage before catching an Ill wind losing itself forever. (Auditory): Ear, or ear Passage. "I feel rough", she said. As I witness, she grows poorly in a

quest to be one in a shell beaten down by the
heaviness of knowledge, holding on to a query
of dreams made true only by freedom.
Freedom from what one knows? No. Freedom
from self, or self in self's current state. "I shall
Bury them", She said. I shall say goodbye less
my choosing Ill afford attendance. Damning
them unforgiven in the hands of ugly
monsters, too large for sight as they fear, trot
on thy foot of such beast angering more, the
demon which bind them. "Never wake me", I
say jokingly, though I rarely Joke. I spout often
truth in a pseudo-smile, in the hopes you have
missed it as I gaze upon your stupid spit
shined teeth placed happily between tainted
lips stained dirty by the tears you gave me as
only a small one. Shall I never forget? Hit me
harder, replaced shouts of my survival now
that I am older. The odd placing's of
untouchable, forbidden marbled lamps strike
thy temple. Split thy cornea blood puddled,
had you hit me as I am, never as I were, nor too
small to realize. A wee chit of a girl could
never inflict such dementia, the courts
shouting, as only I hear them. What had I been
thinking, and would I think it if the moment
arose new the impact of your fist between my
lung and kidney as I mount the stairs leading

to my room? And when Father held me there helping you, decades before full frontal statement of his disapproval of your methods. "He too feared", she said. "Make good old man", I shouted Shit sweat, as she lay crying. And had I kneeled to console her. I now give up my hiding place to ward her off you. Beat us in front of her. Keep her from you, or harming you. Keep her from your renderings, your surprises. Her mouth kept at bay. While praying for your own retrieval of escape, as you long for one with words loaded, packed down. Sweet lead undermining the usual Silver Bullet. And I am alone. I, alone again. Sat, Sitting, Satt-ed. Arms reach-ed behind a screen and a Keyboard. But you may never see me. In fact, you may drive directly past. Duty bound, the weed filled coverlets of a makeshift bed with her by your side loving never her, never yourself, so how shall you love me as she take-up space once spent by mine. Sorry, I were thinking of him, again. Now, where were we? Oh yes and so to Daddy. Dear Father. He too has my betrayed ash upon his sleeve or have I mentioned? While she has yet to leave my side. He, in full aware, my un-be-friend-ability, communicate. My in-ability to survive, as I lean wept by your coffin side and say, O

Daddy, you know that I shan't do this without you. You know that I shan't do anything. How they have housed, kept me, so I may neither except an apology, nor allow them to apologize. She sits proudly, sturdy as steel. Unaware of such stupidity or stripping of her soul somewhere as that child or maybe somewhat older. The entire (80) plus years in Damnation. Someone must have scared the shit out of this poor woman leaving an empty shell. Abrupt to dream must be Sin. Might I add the time reading now (39) past five pm. I, myself just 20.5 minutes ago learned, The Death of Christopher Lee. I myself have over the past 10 odd years leant a sentence per month to what you now read. (Christopher Lee): Sir Christopher Frank Carandini Lee, (CBE), (1922-2015) English Actor, Singer, Author, appearing in over (275) films and a World Record for most Sword Fights. He's helping me. I catch glimpses of past lives beading rolling from me like water off a fresh cleaner wax on a 2015 Black on Black BMW 740 Li. I had a dream of him the other night. He is my Father, as I begged he seek Hospital. In poorly state, he detoured. Walking ahead of me, past A and E, in a Flax colored Mack, Black Ash Walking Stick, and Trilby of a similar. Muttering, as his back and huge stature now face me. ("Get it Done"). I assume he referred to the writing, she said. Writing??, "I suppose", I said. But as you know he scarcely reminded me of Father. Daddy is more your Frank Thornton type. (Frank Thornton Ball):1921-2013; An English Actor, One of my most beloved, Best known for his role as Captain Peacock on a Brit-Com. Are You Being Served. Never the less, Frank is like Father in many ways. Right down to the movement of his head to the breaths he'd take between lines. Mix Frank Thornton, Christopher lee, Peter Cushing, Nickolas Smith, David Niven, and H.B Warner in a Huge Black Kettle, add (2) Puppy dog tails, (1) part Eye of Newt, 1 Tsp. black pepper, a Cadillac Sedan and 1/2 cup pure wickedness. Let boil till thickens. There you have it. Daddy. Picture Victor Newman, Y/R, mid-morning American television. But my sweet Darling Denmon, is, may always be, unlike any living creature over a thousand terms of being. In one of my many, usual, unbearable, seemingly real dreams, I walk. Further out than normal, past the Manor house towards the nearby guest cottage, when I caught sight of a moving figure. Moving in haste, wiping, scrubbing, mopping, twirling, and collecting some large object in a huge white cloth sack. As I moved silently closer, never taking my eyes from the rapid movement. I eventually gained enough closeness to make out his frame and face. Removing now his Dark coke bottle like glasses, placing them on a nearby pedestal, he adjusted his weight to hang the seemingly heavy white sack from a hook which hung trunk from a water ruined ceiling. As I draw closer, now looking into a glass-less window in plain sight of him and his secret, I become frozen with fear as the sack drips heavily with blood. And his ill attempt to wash the constant dripping down a nearby drain proved pointless. His sleeves are rolled, this always frightened me. Dad, wearing an orange and brown checkered shirt, the one from his old photos. As I looked closer, he appeared to be (50) years younger than present. Same as those photos as I began to urinate, in pure hopes the sound of running water would never reveal such deceit. I realized with my usual slowly processing brain that everything in this picture is outdated. The leaded paint, to the wood block on the floors. The glasses, he replaced to his over beading sweat filled brow, decades out of time. Condensate thy very breath holes, as I myself have. The blood just kept coming and soon he gave up, throwing the mop to the floor. Throwing in the towel, he turned to leave. As he opened the door to the right of my viewing, he turned, looked me dead in the eye, then turned to leave, slamming the door behind him. Imagine the fear I felt. The very stare you get, or may have received from your own Father when found engulfed in whatever you know will get you a beating but you had no aware of his observance. Immediately arising from my slumber, terrified. "Had my Father taken the Life of someone, far prior my birthing?", she said, with little known air to lung panting. My birth is (1969). Judging by the era of dress compared to the old photos. This event took place somewhere between the late 50's to early 60's. (RING RING RING) my mobile at half past 8 in the morning. Caller ID,,.. Anyone????? Of course. At the time, I resided in the US. Daddy in Switzerland. The time difference never fazed me as I remembered, he never sleeps. The Man Never Sleeps. Well of course I never answered, would you? I could feel as he knew I knew he knew I knew. "The very source from which my Clairvoyance stems, the old man", she said. Of-course he knows. True Horror. I should have titled this Book, 'True Horror', I told her, as you have now caused hair standing end to end about the back of even my fearless neck. Daddy has always been capable of destruction, this never bothered me before. It were more the level of Psyche, coupled with my heredity that leads me to wonder, Who and What the H@ll I am? She said". I were never to be there. Impossible for me to have been there. I lay yet to be conceived, born. No wonder he fears you, I said. "Me?", she said, with a smile, I have longed for. A smile I had never seen in years. Someone who fears me? How may one believe such non-sense. I bare the scar of the Pitied, never the feared. -"Who am I"?, she asked once more. Now her once never seen smile fades back to shame. How may I have witnessed such Monstrous? A blessing or a curse? No, my freedom proceeds the final splat of gravel upon (2) closed boxes minus (1) sad faced sole. Never wake me, I told her on a full- bottled Wednesday preceding my pre-menopausal state. A time when I seem most Ball-sy, and brash. "NO", I attest. Never wake me, as spirits have", I told them. My not, I attend. My not, in attendance your wake, nor forever sleep. For I may not have forgiven you. Attendance of service is an admittance of forgiveness, as I forgive nothing. Careful how you treat someone, they say, you may well end up looking after them, their children and their grandchildren. And that is the very occurrence damned. Had never I warned them or had they forgotten their promises. (The Critics may now at this point ponder): The Author needs a swift kick in the Backside. They may well say it. What A Spoiled Little Brat. A Daddy's Girl. How correct they are as I stand un-seen patting them firmly on their backs. (Enissophobia): Criticism, or fear of being Criticized. Beauty and Madness? Abuse and over compensation? Old married couples and shall remain as such. "Shun your path to be a Democracy", I said. As I try and deter the conversation. (DEMOCRACY): The Athenians Invented Democracy some 5 1/2 thousand years ago Plato predicted disaster(Credit), Goods offered today, that must be paid for tomorrow. What? she asked in Confusion. "After the (2008) Global economic clash", I continued. Greece declared broke. But the Euro is a wonder-est, exciting thing, Far prettier than the□. USD. (United States Dollar). €. (Euro): The euro, introduced in 2002, New Year's Day. In (2002), Greeks bought Porsche Cayenne more than any other Luxury brand of Automobile. The Euro has a lower interest rate in Greece than

The German Drachma. Greeks purchased mainly Japanese, Italian, and French cars, Porsche, being the most advanced car plant in the world. "You are, AGAIN, wasting your time and mine with useless conversation. "My path is my own", she said. My troubles have teeth large enough to eat your Euros for breakfast...."Betrayal". "Betrayal", she repeated. I asked them and they promised. Dear Mommy and Daddy. "You really must grow past the faults of your parental units", I explained, painfully.

And I walked where no man Hath. I seek-eth my conceivers, my voice echoed, trembling. Ones who shall protect me. Stand strong, never deceiving me. Never striking me, for I may never strike back. Never scolding me, for I may never scold mine. Never caressing me for I am Aphenphosmphobic. Two, who may hold in secret, with great solace, my path which parallel not, the people persons and the overachievers. Instead, walk-eth with me. Amongst the Knower and the un-knowers. The Believer and the disbelievers. Will you accompany me on this hard journey. To a World where man destroys man. Will you witness with me, as man shun his one gift, PRAYER. Placing Fear, Power and Want, his

(3) greatest Sins, on highest hope. And then, before me, shine a blinding light. Striking sharp to char my already tan skin. The pain is great, though I stand un- afraid. I witness, as Angels kneel, wings curled under, as two figures appear, shadowing that bright light. Will you step down with me, my heart sand with stretched out hand. Will you leave a world imagined by needs not, of food, water, shelter, nor air. A World where a mere breath be thy hindrance. Will you accompany me to a World of Popes and Princesses. Where man deceives man. Yet he have-eth no free will except for a belief, he indeed possesses such power. We shall except your challenge, roared the voices like caged lions. We shall accompany you. Keep you safe, warm and sheltered. But only for a short while. And when that bright day come-eth. Promise we not, ye the acclamation, screaming on bended, bloodied knee. But only that you shall kneel quietly. Brow- boned Eastward, As you PRAY (O' GOD), Bless thy Sun and her new born day. For they have caressed we in cradled arms insuring our safe journey home.

(Aphenphosmphobia): The fear of Intimacy.
Never to be confused with (Philophobia): The
fear of Love. "I fear both", she said. Never I
have (since), the bringing of myself, never once
to explain to them the fact that their promises
were never kept. Deadlines, reserves, unmet.
My problem?,,,,, Both parents, born at the
Stroke of Midnight, on their perspective days
of birth. On the Morning of April 7th, 2016,
GOD called for Daddy and he answered. Prior
to (sed) Day. Soon after, Daddy came for me.
On (2) occasions I had to turn him down.
Daddy came for me. Come on, he said. I felt a
beautiful feeling at the beginning of the (5),
sometimes (6) seconds of incredible pain, as
you pass through that thin thread between Life
and Death. The effortless, yet tedious, ever so
aching, pulling from the left corner of your
dying eye. You remember, the one I spoke
about in D'requ-toi Knickers. I felt that
powerful drift to the left, as I struggle to right
my head to the center of my shoulders, the
overwhelming struggle to keep ones self-
awake. I fancy the journey. The feeling is
beautiful. It lay right to the left of me. Just

outside the door of Mitt Rum. I shall not, at this point, ask if you have had the pleasure of reading my prior works. I KNOW, I KNOW, I have stated such prior. But I have grown massively from the time we started and now. I am no privilege. I am honored if you have read them. I shall soon make them more accessible. (Mitt Rum): SVENSKA; Swedish Language, meaning, My Room. The Rain Room. The one in which no evil may pierce. During this struggle to awaken, I jumped to my feet to recover a sleeping laptop and turning on all the lights. I stretched my eyes as far and as wide as I could open them. "I cannot go with you", I remember saying aloud, smiling. I have a Grandchild, and so wish to meet hers. Had I fallen asleep, I would be with him now. Free. Safe. Happy. Back Home with those of which I fit. I remain aloof and uncaring until (2) days after. I received a message from my older brother saying that Daddy had been called. "Oh", I thought. So that's who you were. In full aware of who I am addressing, as always. And always followed by a reply. I understood further, after a conversation with my eldest sister. Who now, at aged (76), has the appearance of a retired Bong Girl. She could easily pass for (40). And though Daddy is (91), passing most times for a mere (45- 50). We are all freaks, she said. SHHHOOOSH, I said. "We caught Daddy's last words", said my sister. "What were they", I asked. Mainly gibberish, she replied. And How he worries about you. "I need somewhere safe for her", he would pronounce, moving in and out of disillusion. I myself, being a Parent. Lucky enough for none, having half of my unsafe state of mind. But if I had such a child, would worry as such. Seeking some form of relief for my ailing offspring, who has never displayed place-age in such a World. Daddy longed for my return to that rightful place. Longing for safe restitution. Worrying the whole life of the child. And Of course, the moment I find a safe warm beautiful place, following my realization between Life and Death, I would immediately long for that very place of sanctum, their placing. Perhaps Daddy realized a space where I fit. Daddy wanted to free me. Daddy wanted to see me safely home. Perhaps he wanted to take me with him. Me and Daddy, being so much the same. Seeing a wondrous place, knowing my pain, finding such splendor and relief. A final answer to all of which I have complained to him. A resolution. If I am happy here, then so shall she be. Is what Daddy must have been thinking. Normal behavior for a caring Parent. Or maybe Daddy were simply returning to that place from which he and I have come. Realizing perhaps. Hey, it is now time to return. "Come on", he said, smiling. It saddens me not, that Daddy has passed. Ok, it saddens me greatly. As it remaining-ly shall. It saddens me not, that Daddy may have had never, his mind upon passing. Seeing as if he had made known his presence alongside me a good (4) days prior. Many a time or just about all the time during passing, the soul or person has gone leaving this shell. This shell that the remaining living who are acquainted have grown rally in mind. Our day never of yet, need such shell till the day of passing arrive-eth. One has often long left the shells we are to burry. What saddens me to a sickness, and with no known cure, is that Daddy knows my pain. Always has and had obviously been seeking my happiness. Now finding a way out for me, I turned him down. I did not go. I would never want for him, to feel as if I had failed again. As he has spent most of my life searching for my relief of unhappiness. Being my Parental unit, longed for an ease of that pain. Finding one. I would have been happy with Daddy or anywhere he saw fit for me. "I

Turned Him Down", she said, weeping loudly. It rips to small slivers, the muscle which has beat-eth these (47) years I have taken ever so for a pebble of life's love and man handling. I only hope that I have not broken his. There is something very special, that I have yet to tell you. Daddy were standing long side my bed, tapping my shoulder as if to wake me for school, as he often had. Well Cross the threshold of blood. The one which no evil shall pass. Recall? What gives me the widest of genuine smiles, is that after years of being told otherwise, Daddy is indeed, of Pure Heart. Of course being my Father would never pay much attention to such a childish fools play to start. The rules would never apply to him, owing to the fact that Daddy would neither frighten nor harm me. So there he lay. Wrapped in the color of Milton. Silk, three times by my Son, his Dad, his Avuncular, my Brother. As the Dutch have compared me to Shakespeare, or he to myself, I had written such for Daddy during our time together in Switzerland. Following a discussion we had about life and Death after a hit and run involving my beloved Feline. This is what I read by his side as he lay in wait his Burial.

TOINEN'S FATHER

AND I WALK WHERE NO MAN HATH.
I SEEK-ETH A CONCIEVER,
MY VOICED ECHOED, TREMBLING
ONE WHO SHALL PROTECT ME
STAND STRONG
NEVER DECIEVING ME
NEVER STRIKE ME
FOR I MAY NOT STRIKE BACK
NEVER SCOLDING ME
FOR I MAY NEVER SCOLD MY OWN
ONE WHO SHALL HOLD IN SECRET WITH
GREAT SOLICE
MY PATH WHICH PARALLEL NOT
THE PEOPLE PERSONS NOR THE
OVERACHIEVERS
INSTEAD WALK-ETH WITH ME
AMONGST THE KNOWER AND THE
UNKNOWERS
THE BELIEVER AND THE DISBELIEVERS
WILL YOU ACCOMPANY ME ON THIS HARD
JOURNEY
TO A WORLD WHERE MAN DESTROYS MAN
WILL YOU WHITNESS LONGSIDE ME
AS MAN SHUN HIS ONE TRUE GIFT
PRAYER
AS HE PLACE FEAR, POWER AND WANT

HIS THREE GREATEST SINS,
ON HIGHEST HOPE.
AND THEN BEFORE ME SHINE A BLINDING
LIGHT
STRIKING SHARP TO CHARR MY TAN SKIN
THE PAIN IS GREAT, THOUGH I STAND
UNAFRAID.
I WITNESS AS ANGELS KNEAL WINGS CURLED
UNDER
AS YOUR FIGURE APPEARS SHADOWING
THAT LIGHT
WILL YOU STEP DOWN WITH ME MY HEART
SANG
WITH OUT STRETCHED HAND
WILL YOU LEAVE A WORLD EMAGINED NOT
BY THE NEEDS OF FOOD, WATER, SHELTER
NOR AIR
WILL YO ACCOMPANY ME TO
A WORLD WHERE MAN DECEIV-ETH MAN
YET HE HAV-ETH NO FREE WIL
EXCEPT FOR A BELIEF THAT HE INDEED
POSESS SUCH POWER
I SHALL EXCEPT YOUR CHALLENGE
ROARED A VOICE LIKE CAGED LIONS
I SHALL ACCOMPANY YOU ON THIS QUEST
BUT ONLY FOR A SHORT WHILE
AND WHEN THAT SEVENTH DAY COMM-ETH
PROMISE ME NOT
YE THE ACCLAMATION SCREAMING ON
BENDED KNEE
BUT ONLY THAT YOU SHALL QUIETLY

KNEEL BROW- BONED EASTWARD
AS YOU PRAY
(O ' GOD)
BLESS THY SUN AND HER NEW BORN DAY
FOR THEY HAVE CARRESSED ME IN CRADLED
ARMS
IN- SURING
MY SAFE JOURNEY HOME

A.S (c) 1985

I proceed to recite proudly. All the while wanting, needing to scream as loudly as possible for Death to release my Dear Father from her clutches. But I were all dressed up you see. My Best of best Frocks, in Black as night black. Hat of a similar material, as its tall crown and short brim are driving me to no end of head splitting tears. My calf muscles done a complete mischief in turmoil, as they twist round one another in seek of relief from what we as women call THE STILETTO HEEL. But my screams were never for pain of clotted blood, but for Daddy, as he lay silently to the rest. Speaking loudly to no other than myself. Joking and laughing to my right ear as we agree to one another. Daddy, I shall discuss with you, at great length, the manner of your appearance here on this great day as I now find your shell 1/4 the size in width from our last meeting. "Of-course Darling, ha-ha", replied Daddy. His often reply following anything that may have flung from my careless, foolish lips, throughout my life as a child and till this very moment. I stood box side at such a length that the others, though never speaking a word or sigh of impatience, wondered if he were their

Father as well, as a line of overdressed, oversize millinery downers quickly formed behind me like a last minute ticket box at Ascot. Had I been gifted with song I would have sang for Daddy. Right down into his lovely box. Something B'jork perhaps. Or perhaps, a chorus of my own admission. "Toinen's Father shall suffice if you search for stature and praise at such an event", she said. Your surprising participation rattled the doubt-y-est of doubters on his grand evening. A well send off for Daddy as he too raised an eyebrow at your ill- attempt to remain silent as always. I had an ill- attend during a family sing- a - long years prior. You remember, those long dreaded winters spent in Ireland. Everyone took a turn. I remain often overlooked. I never speak, so why in heaven's name would I extend the words in song. Now Daddy is gone without ever having witnesses once, a person of strength torn from my limbs and want. Breath nor fear. Never once the balls lay before him by me to do anything. No wonder the man finds his final resting place more of a future destination coupled with the fact that he has left me here with Mother. Damn near middle aged, still, his worries linger from another World. And my dear sister, who to this very day may never speak at my presents nor gaze my direction, for I have chosen never the yellow roses for my very own Birthday Cake Design. O, what a sickening attitude for one to endure. Have I never enough Mental illness on my shoulder? As it rots from its same old- same old average lifestyle. Mother encourages such values in the child. I have never fancied yellow. How ridiculous. "This is the sort of thing I must deal with all of the time", I said. And my sickness from day one, she cannot stand, has grown weary of. Has grown ever so dreadfully tired from. Daddy Has Died. When we first learned of Daddy's Illness, the first thing my sister asked, (IF HE DIES DO YOU THINK HE HAS LEFT US ANY MONEY). I immediately felt sick. MY REPLY, how can you think of money? Daddy were a person far before he became our father. He were a child, a lover, a soldier, a friend, someone's crush. One whom were unlinked. One who disliked another. He lived a whole lifetime. Then one day, after all were said and done, he became our Father. It took we a lifetime to become a part of Daddy's life. He, a complete person, far before we met him. The sad part is that we have never known him. We know not who he is, who he were. We had yet to meet him before he became our Father. We know never the many lives he has led. I would like to get to know him. Today we learned that he may have left a will, insuring we a Huge amount of Capital. More Stress. (HOW MUCH DO YOU THINK IT IS, AND WHY DO WE HAF TO SHARE IT WITH BROTHERS ONE AND 2). The shit that slid from my sister's lips. Our Father is Dead, I said. Why is Capital an issue? I would pay any amount to have one more conversation with the Man. Get to know him. Acquaint myself in smiles we share, the man which Mother has not slandered the whole of our relationship. Show him that I have half way gotten myself together. I then left the room. upon my leaving, mother chimed in saying, well they did more for him than you. then, the moment I left, I could hear her say, it's ok to think this way and do not let anyone shame you out of it. BITCHES. I felt most the dislike of capitalizing any part of that conversation. And wanted it NEVER wasting space in my Book. My mother is to blame for who that child is today. SELFISH, soon to be selfish and alone. She has never been psychologically healthy for any of her children. The other day, I said, now what will we do when you die. In Joking, but remember I never joke. I too, being guilty of saying what others may want to hear for the proper occasion being. Knowing full well that if I attend her departure, shall be dressed for an evening of my awakening. (3) inch heels and a party Frock. (3) inch heels do my calves an acute mischief. Well worth it, for I shall dance the night away in celebration of my freedom. What will we do when you die, I asked in all fakeness. Nothing, her reply, I did not do anything to you-all. YOU-ALL. WOW. So much for English O-Levels. The woman has graced the walls of the U.S for far too many a decades. I remain belted. Silent as always, my eyes in full roll sky-wise. I shall let her have this one, I said quietly to myself. But O what a rude awakening she has before her. The nerve to say such a thing. Is the women really this Big of a fool. This stupid, this un-aware. Had she merely forgotten, or is she a child of pure EVIL. Playing to full account, a game of mischief and lesson. Sad, really. I feel alone. I am Morning my Father purely on my own. When is anything to be important to these people. My Father is passed. Our Father is Passed. Or am I correct in saying MY FATHER? I feel sick. Never again shall I witness as Daddy walks proudly in English made shoes on Thursday, Italian on Saturdays. His German made shoes, His favorites, worn mainly for town. Now, when stood, I wear nothing less than a German hand tanned hide towards the tip of (10) toes. You are the one of my children who would ever care to notice, Daddy would say to me. I have spent the whole of my life waiting for others to see what I see. Now I know that this shall never happen. The clairvoyance, I can understand. But everyday common decency should be a given. What is that poor child to do when Dear Old Mother passes? How shall she breathe when every breath is dictated upon by the Old girl? I wish to never see them again. How disgusting, the manner in which we have been raised. Oppression if ever I lay eye upon. Oppression posed streaks ahead of any historical race related archive. Bother, she never loved my Father. Never have I witness, one ounce of respect towards him. Never has she obeyed a single request. How dare she even think of his pocket or any moneys at a time such as this. The man has been dead a mere (8) days. (8) Days, and...... Sorry, I am having a hard time getting my head around this world in which I inhabit. FILTHY PLACE. FUCK FEAR. (FOR GOD IS GREATER). If I relay this conversation to my sister she may never remember. The poor child has a tendency never to recall important soul clashing events. Today is 4-15-2016. I sit here in full finished-ness of my book, but shall recall my copyright in order to add this very bit. My heart hurts for day. My heart hurts for those who have been stripped of all human decency. I hurt for myself, being of same blood. The lone revelator to ones so far from my own destinies. Here I sit in hopes that you, the reader may have never, your own hurt, and that my book brings peace to those, or at least a feeling of un-aloneness. A feeling of, oh, someone else is going through shit, same as me. Truth is, sad to say this, but it is better to have company, than to wade through shit's creek alone, afraid, or with a feeling that no one else must. There is no such thing as JUST ME. In Laymen's. (LAYMAN'S TERMS): To describe a complex or Technical issue using words that the average individual may understand. "Are you happy now", she said. (AVERAGE): Plain, Normal, Just Okay, Ordinary, Boring, Regular, Common, Mediocre, Standard, Un, or Random. My response when asked a personal question regarding my own personal affairs. You may spend the whole of the night sat awake in brow tangled despair as you try and figure it loose, but never ask, in lieu of comparing me to another. (THERE IS NO SUCH THING AS). All labels, Labels which we, as people, have no right to place upon another, less we have lived another's life. So she sickens of my sickness? A child? A child, born with the exhaust system of a 1974 Cadillac Sedan Deville, with a used carburetor and no muffler tail pipe combination. The samails. Shut the fuck up, I want to tell her. Nothing you say makes any since. You wanted to know what were wrong with all of your offspring, well here it is. You offer no solace, to comment I am always sick? What's the cure Mother? I watched her lose everything from always saying the wrong thing. Ever certain, The Woman, of some instance which has never actually taken place. You say the wrong thing at the wrong time, a fellow classmate once said to me in a 4th grade assembly. Shall I never forget that day. Marvin, something. His surname eludes me. Having been a crush, the striking of his words cut down my heart in triple bypass, stunning me. Burning from my face every hair, every inch of skin. It is from that day, I began to listen to my words before they left my mouth. From fourth grade to age (45) it has taken me on a Long, hard journey to reach back around gripping a singed childhood by the scruff of the neck. Surprising, shocking it. Yanking it backwards as its heels drag upon the ground, ruining her German made shoes she has so creatively boasted about moments earlier. Listen as it screams for mercy. Grasping its neck for all worth, as it may now see me and where it is headed. Oh how I ache for sun and air. The expand is little and afraid with no outage. Where shall the air go if I have little space for it, I would often ask. "You", it yells. YOU, the vile ugly hurt in my chest. Stop your talking now stand before me. If I kill you the air shall follow, awarding you never on past desire but for your release of this poor girl you have followed for ages, in sickness and damn near middle age. I often get the Bends, never near water nor air. I hide my Illnesses to this very day. You are always sick, she says. What an awful thing to say to one gasping for air, when it is she who longs for longing to stand in that very pile of gravel where the assembly hall once stood. Smile, I have arrived. If Marvin could see me now. But to scorn Mother would never bring about change, who now at (81) would haf, yes HAF, to live a second lifetime bringing her to (160) years, before realizing a wrong. NO, she would wither in pain, and offended- ness. This sick beast of burden, my punishment, as I must live every moment of her down (heeval). And she has received such punishment. I watch as her failure remains, only I grow tired of watching it play through. How long is she to live before I am set free. I too wish to un-meet my reserve. Now run and tell my sister, I should say at this point. Like a child on a playground. She's about to borrow the car, she ran to tell her. Really? After permission has been given by the girl, the owner. She's about to cut your Birthday cake. I give (2) bets on one ice shaken never stirred soul that she never expected to find me standing behind her as she swallowed words that cut veins in my very character. "Why would you relay negative views to me regarding my sister"? What I wish to say, as her eyes dilate in size searching for an escape. I may take no more, the shit I have endured for so long and I have no fear of hurting those who have maddened me, Yes MADDENED me. Never underestimate the power of self-Publishing. I write in a state of Madness. Most times screaming for a release as some things I am unable to write. Unable to tell you. I am, on occasion, warned against certain words. I hit backspace more than letters. Hastened against whole paragraphs. My safety threatened by Demons, and the ghost of Madmen. I harbor curtains and drapes cross my door as they stand, unable to cross, peering angrily for one slip up of information wished kept hidden. Fear. "Fear", she cried. I am still the same tortured sole I have always been as I shout "LEAVE ME THE FUCK ALONE", and let me write. See, it is happened again, though I know you cannot hear. Another sentence in deletion. You would have loved it. I wish to stand from you, hairs on the back of your necks. I suppose you will all just have to wait till I am free. Free of my demons. A day that may never come. They do not want me to write, therefore I exhaust myself. I try to concentrate, still they interrupt me. At times, I find myself beginning again. Starting over. How I wish to write without looking over my left shoulder." Release me", she cried, release me for I am free, or so I sure think. Some days I may find I can adorn my own bedroom doors wide open, my back to them. This is another of such, on many occasion such as yesterday, my thresh hold remain tight in curtain and tails with little known peep upon my person by stranger, monster nor troll. I can feel them and they know it. It is a game you see. A child's game. As I have said (b4), they may never cross. They merely lay an ever-so ailing contentment with the unwilling yearn to never stare at one who holds deep, a power may jest me, as well as they. Yes, JEST. " Ridiculous", I say in all contempt. Hath there no louder sound Than Prayer? "It is time for a new beginning", I said. Time for positive thinking. The World has many options, much to offer one such as yourself. You have a great mind. It should be put to positive use. Teach, never revealing too much. Preach, without changing your religion. Smile without thinking of your past, Love without fear of heartbreak, learn to lean on others in times of need, without feeling the fool you once were. "I shall, someday", she said. Till then, I have mother. A woman who may never leave me alone. "Let go", I say. You are a woman of an age, yet you insist on remaining a groaning mouth, full of regret. "Never release me from her grasp, allowing me to breathe freely on my own", she continued.. Daddy lives (100)'s of (1000)'s of miles away, still his fears, conjuring's, and diluted love follow me. Forcing me to change time and time again, my mobile number. I have fucking had enuff (ENUFF). I wish never to awaken again in this place. I wish never again to see these walls. I wish never again to feel the pain of my captures, with their hard knuckles and harsh words. I want what others have or work hard for. A regular Job, Friends, an Apartment with a kitchen and a Bathroom, Bills, an Automobile in a garage that opens during daybreak setting fourth me and that vehicle, duty bound for business. (8) Hours making a change in the world. But how must I get on with others in a normal world when I see, know, relish, conceive more than normal. I know the hearts of men as they pass me on the street. I know jealousy of co-workers as they make hard for me to earn a wage. I see it coming before it is thought, before they wake. I am a Freak of nature. An Alien amongst the Humans. A painful blistering wart on the heal or heel of mankind who has never been allowed to want, fear, ask, cry, hurt, feel, or show happiness. You do not need a life, Mother would always say. Stay here with me. Stop wanting a nice life, there is no such thing. Something I have and would never say to my own children. No wonder they have moved on, found friends, love, homes, dreams, careers. Happiness. How proud I am of them, never bearing, inheriting the heaviness of weird-om. (Wierdom) or wierdom-ness. Thro this off mother would say, (YES, THRO), nor could I ever want more than my knowledge and Secrets. Replace knowledge with happiness? No, never in this life or any other. For I shall remain POOR, ALONE, UNBEFRIENDED, UNHAPPY, UNLOVED, UNEMPLOYED, ON PUBLIC TRANSIT. (POWER): SIN. (KNOWLEDGE): Sin?. NO. Never when used wisely. In which case one holds very little knowledge, whatsoever. The time read, 9:19 am, and there were a dead fish floating on the Detroit River. "Only one"?, I asked. It is THAT Sin. You know the one. Damn. "I, at current hold it firmly on the tip of my Clyde and (5)", I said. It is the one between Fear and Power. Something to do with being Doxophobic.

(DOXOPHOBIA): The Doxophobe, One who fears Praise.

''To a H@ll with fear, she said. Would have allotted we a Best Seller. "No one's impressed with your Nigga Schools", she shouted leaping towards me, again, snarling, with fingers and claws. Best keep it below bottom lipped theories before divulging our ages to passersby. The time is now 4PM and I Fancy a (6) pack of Fine English actors. In case I wear the first 5 out. How I praise The English Actor and the Rainy days which adorn them. How Beautiful a rainy day. The sort which darkens the home, causing the use of electric lite, yes lite. Do I really need (GH) for such a simple sounding word? GEEEZZ., "Bugs me", she says, rubbing her hands together. "Tires my fingers", as I agree. A chance to rite, yes rite, no (W). My word, how confusing a World in which we land. Complicated, yet tiresome. Are you (FN) joking? I asked one critic. Have you never yet, the Jest of my book? The RAINY day is one of Nature's Gentlemen. Then read it twice. "Read it Jaw to Sternum before insulting me", I say this time round. My un hidden Accent in hand. Angered to the point of forgetting who I wish to hide from being shall anger me far past the point of destruction to thy muscles after the stroke. Learn the meaning of life in treu form, (TREU). Pay me in rotation due distribution. Let her live as I have Died. Now about your busy world in hastened your own tiny world full of need, want, greed and The Taunt of those who lay in wait of accusals and dissatisfaction, poor diction corrections, and the refusal of publication. I know all too well, hurt, refusal, and turned-down-ness. We played together as children.

We grew up together. I have tired of my journey with little time left. We fade. My hands. It is my hands I shall miss. Our hands, our most worn of tools. What we see the most of. The things we have seen more than any. More than our feet. More than our loved ones. More than our faces which require aid of mirrors. More than our sky, the clouds. The rain, my gallant lover. My Hands. Soon they lay crossed my chest, stiff, yet cuffed in prayer. But I shan't see them. "It were me", she said, It were me you saw dressed as that cigarette in that Banana Leaf Water Hyacinth box where I lay faced upward. Me. My smoke, my friend. What else have I to look forward to, yet again, never upon praying hour. Or is it the smoke which hath take-eth me? There is such an art to smoking cigars. Especially the (2) for a pound packs. "UT-Oh", I thought. One of many tall tale as told by She. They should be well seasoned for total optimum taste. Start with a whole piece if the hour is 10pm, no earlier. Puff (6) to (10) good draws. Followed at 10:30, puff the same. 10:50, (4) long draws to the back of the throat. 11:30, (6) long draws. 11:50, (4) draws to the back of the throat. Place in a cool dry place till morning. By 8am you shall achieve the best half inch dried to perfection inexpensive smoke of your life. Should you require smoke between 11:50 and 8am smoke the second one. But break it in half first only puffing the top portion as your tongue is expecting something stronger. (Swisher Sweets Regular (2) pack). As for the Davidoff (3000) needing no seasoning, puff at will. But only in public. No point in having something great if there's no one there to see it. I, being of a somewhat, Superstitious Nature, have seen fit to toss mine having puffed to hard landing it hot ashes and all to the back of my throat. "Somewhat"? Once moisture seeps in, it is over for me. I should have lay-ed it flat, Yes Lay-ed. Letting it dry, though the act of such may well bring about bad luck. "What a waste", I thought, as I now must survive another, nothing filled day in haste of my coveted fumes. Never to mention, first smoke of the morning is magical, be it as the throat is dry. Of course, you do know they shall eventually DESTROY me. But Only after I am diagnosed (LOL). The Doctors shall blame Cancer, my Family shall blame the Doctors, I shall blame anyone who did not purchase this book, and so forth and so forth. Why are mere mortals to blame for the Death of one another when in all reality, we merely die on our day of Death. Or, between you and me, or you and I, depending the mood I am in, usually one week after we are actually taken. If Cancer is the blame of my passing, please never cast sentence, locking it away. Less you are certain it may well bring about my resurrection. An action I am sure none of the Dead agree upon. I have, on occasion the privilege to experience many forms of the hereafter. All forms of animation, for instance. The drawn ones, The puppet tune. Lego Land, now that's a big one, nearly impossible to navigate. I witnessed a man as he has passed, now he is a tulip. A very large tulip condemned to a watering can of warm water for an eternity as he smiles brightly eyes closed. His face tilted slightly towards the Sun. Had I never witnessed such, I may never have become aware as my Brother's, yes, the same, as well as my Sister's Prayers for my very Freedom. My very Mental wellbeing, as I had so Prayed for their Happiness. "May one never trap a mouse, nor swat a fly", she said. Heaven knows who you are sending into yet another form of Human Life. "Heaven may", I say. All forms of Life and Death who remain, we should know by now, are synonymous. The very creation of such, so called entertainment for children and adults alike, is an abomination or the witness of one not unlike myself. Perhaps ignored. Perhaps trapped in a world never of his or her origin. SUCH AS MYSELF. Deemed Crazy. What are we to do upon then realization of having been thrown into an unknown World sept to try hard and inform through words and illustrations. We often go unnoticed or highly praised. "Never somewhere in between", she said. Death is confusing at first, to those who know not what it in tales. Paaid full my dilly-anting, she said, Paaid, with (2) small A's, looking sourly at her right hand and left forefinger. My rings, she whispered, my beloved Lois Hills. What shall become of them? They have held me and kept me warm for many years. Shall I take them with me, she asked. No. I think I shall remove them, or have they already been removed? Are they tucked neatly to their boxes or are they proudly worn by my Daughter and hers? Does she think of me when she looks down? When she is cooking, or driving. Do they pass her eye as the sunlight strikes a granulation or am I just forgotten? I have left them nothing. I have made nothing of this name. Nothing for them to have or cherish. Just silly old Momma. I were their Mother. They Loved me. They said it often. But I never amounted to much. Have never been allowed to. I never knew how to, as they say, Handle (Yo- Bid-ness). Go for yours. I remember now. I remember as a child, I could never get mine. The other kids got it, not me. Therefor I had to scramble to figure it out. I remember in 3rd grade, we were asked to write a report. Read the story and give our thoughts. But even as a child, writings and Novels seamed pale in compare to what I knew. If I read it, I had already experienced or felt as if the Author(s) were rewriting my own life. I felt as if he or she was boasting about things I had already known to be true and they were somehow following me. I sometimes felt anger at the publication of their words, while mine remain stuck in my head, eager to get out. Set free, so that someone, somewhere would see me for greatness and remove me from the clutches of my Parents and I would never have to go there again. I could smile and be free like other children. I did not comprehend, and as we were told to leave our reports in a file till the next day, I can remember taking a neighbor's paper, and filling in my own name. Watching shamefully as she searched for it to no avail, ultimately starting a new one. Getting even further than the first, while I sat holding a paragraph written by someone else with no book worth. Merely my worth and worry of the world, and what I could do as I grasp this tiny planet in my hands, unable to grasp my own life. "And now look at you" she said. "You have written a whole book,,,,,,, or something". "I now realize that I am still this way", I said, ignoring her sarcasm. I never mixed well with this human breed. I were far too busy watching, as laffers (LAFFERS), and passers by learning to deceive one another. Oh yes, at as young as 3rd grade the two in one person were fast at work. One engaging in conversation, the other standing to the side, showing true feeling. I could see this, it astonished me. The hurt arise-eth later behind founding myself as the only one who could see it. "THERE IS NOTHING ON THIS PAPER", shouts the retched Mrs. Beezio, for all to hear.

(Embarrassment Phobia): We are still searching for a name. If you know of such, Please, feel free to Email. Better still, write us.

BETTER STILL,,,Let me Name it. Oh, I do not know, shall we call it BEEZIOTEACHEROWEREABICHOPHOBIA? Meaning; My 3rd grade professor Mrs. Beezio is a Bitch and I hope she is currently choking on a hot acidy, gastric bloods, puke mixture at this very Moment. But why could she never, an adult, see what I had seen. (2). One person plus his double. The real and the fake. The knower and the un-knower,,,, COM- ON- U- NO WHTZ- NXT; The Believer and the Disbeliever. Now you're catching on. I cried for days at my misfortune of having been born extraordinary. What a shitty break. It pays nothing and has always payed Nothing, Zero, Nil, Not. NO, I have never gone for mine, so to speak. There were many obstacles which blocked my path of human life. I have never gone for, nor have I ever been taught to live in the world which I had been born. You're not like them, Mother again. If you teach a child what you teach them, they grow up to be what you have taught them to be. ©2013 "No longer", she said, and now it is too late. I have felt the flutter dropping me to the bottom of something, though I remain. "Is this what death feels like?", I asked, Terrified, in my loudest voice, seeing that she is now further away than normal. The room has tripled in size and she is too far to make out my words. "Is this it?", I shout across the room at her. Am I to go on? Am I tucked to my end, black box and under-lay? Am I wrapped (3) times in white? Are they sad? Do they wonder where I have gone?

Do they believe that I am no more, as I continue the life I have with the same fears, the same Loved ones, in this same nasty place, only with the ones out of the (2) parts who know and accept death's side? While their human halves mourn my passing, heartbroken at my departure. I, lucky to have merely fallen asleep as we all are. If we feel great pain, great fear, we live to tell, but it shall never precede death. As one slain boy once said to me, I only remember falling to sleep at the residence of an uncle. During my life I remember feeling great sadness at the news of his historic passing. The brutality, the state of his body. I never told him. Nor had I shown him the news clippings of an open casket for all to see. I would have done, though could never figure if it would be my chastisement or his for him to know or be told. I realize now that nothing is real sept for GOD. Nothing we see,,, touch. The people, memories. The World. This life, our families. Nothing is real. Prayer is real, God is real, nothing else. Remain Calm. "You shall be fine", She whispered in my left ear. And as I leaned (9) days toward (46), I could hear her clearly, as if she were standing next to me. Now I watch and listen as she and her voice fade slowly into nothingness. Give up this search for Life, she said. You have yet to be Born. Had my heart beat-eth prior to this very moment, it, at this very moment, may well cease to. Perhaps it were She who hang bleeding from Daddy's white sack at its drip. She has since left me, never to return. She has gone. My search for her remain nil. Abandon me now? As I think aloud. I search profusely, in my Apoplectic state.

(APOPLECTIC): Angered to the point of Stroke.

 I have yet, at present to lay less than my half eye upon her than a bat in the sun. I too miss her hands. Now on my own, I feel I shan't be able to grasp what I, in that 3rd grade class found impossible to conceive. A life of my own. Far too late. It has been, what I believe to have been some (38) years now. But I must return, though the school has long been reduced to a pile of stones. Had it ever stood? I must return to the moment when I realized who we are, as certain whom I want to be. Shake her as hard as I dare bringing she back from her dazed state, allowing me to progress and live a normal life. I fancy simple things. O where can she be? 1/2 a fortnight as I watch outside our humble number (9). I stare in tear stains wonder and invisibility at myself as I go about life and its lie. My human side about its business, as our Son hurry about his day. Charging his car (b4) drifting off. She, spending most of the day in tears for her loneliness and lack of activity. Unaware of our fate, for I have since left. God may never throw one beneath a train dropping a heavy flag poles upon body releasing thy soul. He sends love to the rescue when it comes you follow, unable to tell the ones you love. Watching as the misunderstood believe there is a difference between Life and Death. All the while holding hands with their unhuman side, as they too watch themselves cry at your wake. Ever smiling and alive in pure full belief. I recall my realization of no longer inhabiting my human form. I could ride thru a puddle on the ground seeing tracks by previous riders and wonder why my wheels left no track. It angered and confused me at first. Frustration, resulting in a second ride thru, still nothing. I began to feel out of place in crowds. No, never my usual un-want- out of place among Earth bound creatures. Pitting the fact they stand on queue.

Most aggravating as I find myself ignored in popular book haunts apart from stares by number-less souls atop the highest shelves in the children's section. O, how they lounge to gaze at me for hours never reading one page of anything", I recall. The very reason for cats in a bookstore. Spirits. How their eyes follow my every move. Disguised as Millionaire Tramps dawning their finest Ralph Laurens, delightfully frightening forcing my soul to flee and never return. Shall I do as such, I asked. Shall I behave, do well at such an interview. That is but all life is, an interview for the real World. Most fail as I have. Most pass. Shall we do well on one's own? I cried bent weeping, all the while longing for the ensemble worn by the kid with the bright blue eyes tanned skin and platinum locks sat atop the Dr. Seuss plush toys. How far well must we grow before encountering infancy? How then does one provide when one is so well provided for? I fumble towards such days which followed, alone. (Ralph Lauren): Ralph Lauren is an American clothing designer and founder of what became an iconic global brand. "Can I do this on my own?" I cried bent, weeping. Longing for the shoes worn by that kid with the startling green eyes atop the Mystery section as I wonder if they even come in my size. Again, I ask, how must one grow before encountering infancy? How then, must one earn when one has been handed everything? How must I provide, when I have been provided for all of my life? (Repetition) I slip through the days which followed, side by side with myself. Before a night of suffering. It is the Bends, again. Brings about such pain that thy only relief be Prayer for sudden Death with a cheery wave bye- bye to those which you cherish. (THE BENDS): Decompression sickness (DCS; also known as divers' disease, the bends or caisson disease) describes a condition arising from dissolved gases coming out of solution into bubbles inside the body on depressurization. DCS most commonly refers to problems arising from underwater diving decompression, but may be experienced in other depressurization events such as working in a caisson, flying in, unpressurized aircraft and extra-vehicular activity from spacecraft. Considering I have stood, standing in this very spot for the odd (47) years, my condition is Diagnosed as an over-active burnout syndrome caused by closed in recycled air. (Claustrophobia): Fear of confined spaces. My fear of Pain, or (Anglophobia), has found me

scrambling for Tylenol 3 with Codeine, and a
swallow of Heinz Apple Cider Vinegar, chased
with a tea temperature china tea cup of hot
water in my final seconds of motion before the
all familiar Paralyzing intermission of such an
affliction takes hold. I, just minutes prior
pleasure French inhale a half inch of Boog-aloo
-Spliff, a Swisher Sweet mini, ingested (2) cups
Southeast Australian Cab/Sauv, (2) Bayer
Aspirin, and 1 (RX) grade Benadryl. In hopes
to overt, or elude the on-coming misery I knew
all too well. (CAB/SAUV): Cabernet
Sauvignon; French. One of the World's most
widely recognized red wine grape varieties.
But instead of my usual body-stiffening agony,
I experienced complete numbness with an over
whelming need to stand or at least roll from
my present position. There is a great presence
over my head towards the door of my room of
my very soul overtake-eth if not for an
overpowering pull of will from my fear and
own safe keeping which may keep me safe
from what I cannot see. If unspeakable
presence were to reach me would rip me to
shreds. Imagine my fear as I long to run and
hide but may never move. Then I stretched to
remember in my numbed state about the
blood. Whatever Desires me inhabits pure evil,

pure evil indeed. I finally pulled my soul free from my lifeless body fleeing to a nearby room where my Son sat totally engulfed in the X-BOX 360 version of GTA 5. Now locked in total safe-a-tude, or were I, as he could neither hear, nor see me. I hesitate to scream at first, owing to the fact it lay common for a man never to notice the world coming to an end during a game of GTA. In desperation, I screamed. I even attempted to hide behind him, grab at his shirt. I shall take a chance on The ultimate NO NO,,,, Knock The Controller From His Hand. Still nothing worked. I appear to be invisible to all but you. It is as if I were not in the room at all. (TRUST ME, I COULD TELL THE DIFFERENCE FROM WHEN I AM USUALLY BEING IGNORED DURING A TREVOR COP SHOOTING SEQUENCE). Someone, or something pursued me, in long search of me. It's bleeding teeth, feasting on my flesh. Craving more from its favorite dish and nothing would stand between IT, and the cracking of my bones beneath its feet. As I squealed for a hiding place, I could hear what sounded like high tapped heels to that of a New York follies dancer left back stage, turned rejected by it is title suitors and directors. Warned to leave, instead to stay reeking torture on the likes of onlookers and set designers in a whirlwind of deceit and revenge. The footsteps grew closer as to have been heard down a long corridor towards me. Her feet, her shoes. The first things to catch a half eyed sick in state girl. How beautiful her shoes, the main subject on my mind. Her dress, same as the one I had earlier tried for size from a reduced rack at a downtown Anthropologies. Stockings, sheer, in Blackest Black imaginable wrapped in untouchable Vellum, beauty and refinement. Her hair in up-do-ed magnificence. Nails sharp, clean, bare, and would fair princess envelope a bodily function, would leave neither smell nor stain upon the finest of pure White Handmade Burmese Rug. (As I write this, recreate this, the sickening memory find myself doubled over in Pain, sick to my stomach finding it impossible to compose a standing, or correct sitting position comfortable (enuff) to hit a backspace key), A WHISPER B-TWEEN YOU, THE READER, AND MYSELF. On realization we share the same face as I am looking in a mirror coveted by a Puff the magic dragon cloud when we see who we truly are or truly want to be. She is me and I am terrified. Oh no, Now I Recall. It is SHE, in truest form. No sadness, pure confidence. No more dirty gowns drenched in snot and tears. And with one hand round my throat it grasps. Lifting me from the floor and over a black pit, which somehow hides in the bowels of my Son's man cave. Having no prior knowledge of it, I seem aware from move in day. Being of a Clairvoyant Nature, one sees everything. But to oppose my belief on each obstacle of my brain rotting gift, would draw from me more time than (sed) illness. Never to mention I felt it was to him, no danger. Holding me over such a dank filthy pit she spoke, and I quote, "(You Tried To Kill Us)", End Quote. "No," I replied, with short supplied air to my Pharynx. The pharynx is a muscular tube lying behind the nasal cavity and mouth, carrying air from the nose toward the larynx and food from the mouth toward the esophagus. (Health Hype.com). I now find myself in hand begged glory as I declare un-dying Love to no other than myself. "No, I say to no avail. I Love You, US. " BUT I DO love You", I yearn to repeat as loudly and as many times as I could muster. As She has shown zero emotion, no sweat glands, no pores, no sigh of life, just beauty. Pure beauty and nothing else mattered. Why the fact alone, that she were standing in my dirty UN welcoming shit hole of a habitat made little less difference to a being with no thought sept the bent-ment on my destruction. And in a moment before unconsciousness, I realized she is who I had longed to become the whole of my miserable stench of a life. Her strength, confidence, perfection, zero body fat, (no exaggeration on my part). Shiny blue- black hair, lack of self-doubt, lack of fear, disbelief. The sinner within me envy thy enemy. Thy very beast of my lifelong confusion. And where were she when I needed her, as I cower in corners in fear of the day, the night, and the (4) foot path to my lunch when I feared judgement from others awaiting my company at that same dinner table. Why have you hidden from me, I want to ask her but cannot for I fear her as I fear myself times (10). And as she extend her arm to drop me pit bound to h@ll's cold await, I noticed, Bare arms?,,, She has no tattoos. "Don't Hurt Him", I scream in fear for my Son, locking one eye on him, one eye on she, my third eye to ponder why she had no birthmark on the right shoulder when mine reads, (9). An ever most irregular mole. (9) shaped of the number itself. Being a bit of an ego maniac, I, in my earlier years saw fit to alter to its true form. " I would never harm him, I am his Mother", she said, in angered, h@te devoured state, as she lowered me to my feet staring Mad Man style to my eyes before she turned to leave, never to return. The sound of her stilettos faint now as I search desperately for my room where my body lay. I am careful to see that she has truly gone so as we may never more lock a half eye in case she changes her mind. The house seems larger, corridor longer, further away and impossible to navigate. SLAM,, I hear in a distance. She has gone. Am I safe now, I wonder as I slowly seep from the sound of Trever on that damn motor cycle. Darkness from a door appears. My room. Dark, zero visibility, the way I like it with it is black walls, and unfinished Wedgewood floors. I see my body, tattoos and all, as I lay flat on my back, left arm crossing my chest. I rush breathless in disbelief toward it as I awaken shit faced in fear filled 100% aware of what has just taken place. And in total doubt dropping truth this having been a real occurrence, never a dream. And thoe, YES THOE. And thoe, she has gone, I could hear her voice as if I were speaking to myself. What? I pondered leaning towards the floor in hopes to empty my bowels and stomach, sending me into a state of absolution or relief of the overwhelming heat thrown round my resurrected flesh in a pool of whatthefucknessdidijustmeetmyalteregoism.? WHAT-THE-FUCK-DID-I-JUST-MEET-MY-ALTER-EGO-ISM). (Hippopotomonsterosesquipedialiophobia): Fear of Long Words. LOL. And if She is me, or I am She, why fear anything, big or small. The emotionless female would have taken on Trains and Giants for me, so where has she been? Why has she hidden in silence at the times when I needed her most. Days when I stood frozen in fear. Words which have gone unsaid. Cutting words. Sharp edged Dick sized knives on the backs of bullies whom would have stood motionless in wait of her reply. Still nothing. Where were she? Never one phobia saw, seen, unseen. Thought, upheaval, dare rear its head, as she pranced her fancy ass up and down the un-washable walls of an ill forsaken passage towards my tiny lone stricken brain cell. You know, the one with the eviction notice. Why, if she. She who has feared nothing. She, whose flawless skin grazed robes fit for a King along the filth where I inhabit without a care. Why, if she were with me all the while, and had I known she were there, would have never known fear. "Why,, I am the great pretender", she answers through me proudly. Towering away my years in your fancy clothes, Judging you. Jester me pretending to care, all the while Praying in great and only hopes that my words, my very hopes need never slob upon your shoes. We all come with titles. Even Kings yearn for purposes, heroes and guidance. Poor, poor Animals, the squad leaders we take for granted. Dog, man's best friend? You have no idea. The family feline, ever alert. Warding evils some may never see. Spitting at nothing to a dark corner between the closet and exit were we may see only hinges. The loyalty of a dogs bark sensing trouble. "Who are you". "Why me?", I asked, Why me. Why wait so long? A tortured soul damned in fear, head down, eyes pooled. My forever frozen Cardiac rounding in single digit. You have stood, standing, waiting since my earliest days. My unchanged illusion less torment on wet, dirty floors where you could have helped countless others or many like myself. (Automysophobia): Fear of Being Dirty. The heat greatens, as She draws nearer yet unseen. If I allow another to dampen your touch what part of you may I call my own? "Soon", I stated. Soon you shall realize who we are. I shall wait forever for that day. "How may I, the weight of an Apostle with no kitchen. How am I Disciple, through improper Shatting. How then must I tantrum angrily to shatter with wings of Angels? How was I to save Mankind with no stable restitution and no come down? And if I had lived as Kings do, how would I have cared? A Grandfather clock, my wrist watch. The highest of towers, my leaning post. The steepest mountains, a mere hill. Waxed marbled boxes, a confinement were I crouch pleading to stretch cramped legs. A Stucco sculpted, vaulted ceilings open thrice daily, yes Thrice. Feeding on vegetation, now sculpt oil canvas and scripture left for Art by men of Loud and Silent Knowledge. (Muhammed). Yahya Ibn zakariyya (Jean Baptist), Homer, Peter the Great and others. Humanitarians, Thinkers, Kings, Inventers, Philosophers, Scientist, Religious Leaders. "They would often visit me as a child", she said. As I grew older the meetings grew less frequent. I never knew them, though they knew me. Never knew what they meant, till now. Who were we. Are they visiting, as I am. When shall this journey end. What have I learned. What shall I report, when I have neither preached nor taught. Neither led nor founded. Neither designed nor invented. My time spent Pled, yes Pled. Tell me I too am

no Immortal. That I too may pass. I have sense
returned to Daddy's cottage in the grounds.
Entering, walking through those puddles of
blood. I approached the dripping white sack,
releasing it from its confinement to catch a
glimpse inside. What my eyes lay upon
astound me, for it is no other than me. Me,
myself, I. My very body and soul. Alive,
smiling. My (2) hearts sliced (9) times open in
full outpour spill the whole of my fears. I am
free. (40) plus fears and phobias Bleeded. YES
BLEED-ED. Outward and onto the floor down
a no longer disputing to look upon, rusted
drain. Daddy has spent, what appeared to be
decades upon decades in the hopes of my
healing. The whole of his time spent, cleaning
up my mess. Covering my Ass. And His
apparent toss in the towel. Merely Daddy's
passing. I had not seen the past, but the past
present and future. "Daddy, covering my bum
until his day comm-eth''. She said. And as the
last drip drop-ed, I gasp my last gasp. I am
now truly free. Free from Fear, Want. Now all
may become clear. Who am I? I am the
Pluviophile, lover of The Rain. I am the
Anglotope for I love England and her ways. I
am Giants on whose shoulders the Great and
Self-Righteous stand. Libraries, Museums, once

my home. Hundred foot statues my clothing hang to dry. Domed glass ceilings which nourished my Sun charred skin now house pools and gardens of the rich. Wood carved water crafts, my shoes. My Tiny Toy Trains now Tower to crush me in greatest un-screamable fear. All the while laughing in ear shot of that beautiful cracking sound as my bones have crumbled to dust. I am the Siderodromophobic. Who am I?,,,,,, I am all which you Fear, I am All which you Desire. I am the one who never sleeps.

You, my dear girl, are THE OTHER ONE: (Finnish): TOINEN. Der Geschichtserzähler. The Story Teller. O, how I have Harbored thy sweet dear Mental Illness. YOU CHARLETON. Sticky, foul beast which exhaust me so, as she pull from one to another. And my souring soul. Back, now forth between truth, belief and reasoning. Right, wrong. What I shall, nor may never say. (SAY); My least favorite word, in all the languages. For Decades, it has been I who have watched as you devour and destroy. It is I, who lay dormant watching as you Nash sharp teeth at Love. Betrayed by you, as you turn my Dear Brother to stone and stick. Confining him to a loveless cold and unwanted heart at the mere sight of me. And now his smile brings a kind warmth to surround my very own heart. His happiness invites me to safe places where Love has overflown, leaving enough to share with his World and our past has been blinded by such. It is YOU. It has been you the entire time. YOU, who shun kind words, turning them to a place of solitude, greatness less not and means of other meanings to harm me. But It is I who have PRAYED. As you left us single handed at the World's door where others have entered with no avail. While others played, laughed. It is I who leap forward to hit brick and mortared wall, as you took never to give back even a damns worth of affection. Emotionless, as we walk hand in hand, side by side. Then soon after, one in one. It is I who lay afraid as you push aside all rebound of friendship coming's. Keeping me to you, holding me near. It is I, Us, You, We, the girl with (2) brains. Our time has come-eth, dear child, as I release you releasing all fear. And my loves lovely slamming of that door. Thy very exorcism returning me to our parlor near the North facing window overlooking our childhood yard where my Dear Brother lay reach for sibling loves embrace as you push him away, striking downward his face, fattening his lip. We were but mere children and his eyes were glad to see me. I searched for you Dear Brother as I have not found you. Just an empty lot lay in dirt hills and stones for you are no longer there. There, where she first possessed my soul. And to your confusion our Mom and Dad (reeeek). That's fine, said Mother as Daddy say nothing at all. She does not want a hug right now. Sending you to the head of the line of a lifelong confusion of WTF is wrong with my kid sister. Why have they never looked after him, I wondered. But you are not here as I stare where naked walls and unfurnished rooms would have stood. Now I remember. We have grown far past this and all I need do is send a text in await your smiling reply. I alone set forth my soul, free from my confinement. Free from this place. I step proudly now my big toe cross rotted thresholds and uncrossed paths, allowing Daddy to rest. As I shall one day accompany him to that glorious place of which he has so raved. And our poor, Dear, Sweet Mother, who you so take as beast on abuse and harshness has so conditioned you to withstand, never merely this interview you call life, but any H@LL imaginable, as you have walked through screaming, where others have merely fallen face first giving in to the same H@LLS.

Who Am I?

I AM THE ORIGINAL.

I am SHE.

I am (Greed, Poverty, Hope, Absolution, then Death).

I AM, Nikn AHSffitch Lovsangare.

I am The Willow Warbler".

END

Nikn): (Greek:): Νίκη, "Victory", pronounced,
(NIKEE), goddess who personified victory,
also known as the Winged Goddess of Victory.
Roman equivalent Victoria. Depending upon
the time of various myths, she, described as
daughter of the Titan Pallas, goddess Styx,
sister to Kratos (Strength), God of War, Bia
(Force), and Zelus (Zeal). NIKE, Same as the
shoe. Pronounced: (9), Nine.

(A.H.S. ffitch): AHSffitch; (with 2 small ff's):
Pronounced (OWZ-VIK),

(A) Alien.

(H) Has.

(S) Surfaced.

(f) fear addicted. (f) forgotten.

(i) Impossible.

(t) To.

(c) Capture.

(h) Her.

(Lövsångare):,,(Lovsangare)Svedish:,(Svenska), Swedish, Meaning: Willow Warbler: (Phylloscopus trochilus), Phylloscopus, common widespread leaf warbler breeds throughout northern as well as temperate Europe. Asia, from Ireland east to the Anadyr River basin in eastern Siberia. When this bird performs, all question vanishes, with regard to the willow warbler. A definite agreement of enjoyable notes which constitute a genuine song. I had pleasure to witness one of these creatures on the Isle of Mull. (ISLE of MULL): Scotland's Fourth Largest Island, Mountain Range, fourth largest Island surrounding Great Britain. (MULL); Gaelic.

Niknahsffitch Lovsangare: (9-owz-vik-lov-zin-gara). Mother to Asante S. Rajda, and Louxoi Shane. Grandmother to MiMi S. Rajda.

Had MY BOOK been A FILM....

I would write it, die before it is done. Quebec
Born Cinematographer-ed Camera Pan of a
well-Manicured hand, Lifting the book from a
clean marbled surface while only a trained eye
or avid movie goer or critic spots a poster of
this very Novel in the distance which reads,
Best Sellers list. Book signing today Only.
Crowds. Many voices, Book Shop. All the Press
Abound. A voice, hand and Microphone
appear., " What is your inspiration for this
book", ask an unknown actor, character, Lead
Reported. This is it, he thinks. Set to mark
upon history, his (10) minutes of fame in the
hopes of his own starring role. She who has left
me would emerge as the camera pan from the
hand to the face showing. You Know, in all her
glory, smile. Jump to Black screen. Payroll
credits, simultaneous with dangerously good
hard based strong music, (Lupe Fiasco).
Choking, chest arresting bass beats at the
chorus, (Dumb It Down). Leaving you the
audience with cramped legs and gas as your
bodies digest stale popcorn, nachos and cold
slushies'. Stretching now your arms over your
heads to right your back muscles for the on
putting of your wraps and the drive home. OF
course, the opening credits, accompanied by

Sound Garden's Spoon man. Or better still, Stuff the rock, give me a full on Danny Elfman composition throughout. P.S. Minus the Film, Music and other BS, you've no proof of the story's actual ending. No Hero Music, PLEASE. And Certainly, NO CELEBRITY Cameos.

Thank You

EMPORTANT

There are those, who are out to get me. Those
of whose main objective is to destroy literature,
such as mine. Some even of common Blood.
Using alternative names. Names which Father
has, in the past, used to disguise my identity in
the hopes of insuring my safety, well-being.
Yet I remain related to none and not. I am the
Mother of my offspring and theirs. The only
family in which I lay claim. My certificate of
Birth, so rightly states,
NIKNAHSffITCHLOVSANGARE. If words I
say sounds familiar to you, a lot of my secret
information has been leaked. Apart from
numerous advances towards publishing
houses, the odd Literary Agents, who seemed
to find fault with every word, though secretly
longing for drool over what they could have,
would have, should have written. Had they
been similarly informed. Sending me head first
into the realm of self-publish-ment. Daddy's
story too, has been read before. The year I
spent in the (US). Midwest, of all places. I
produced a small publication entitled The
Michigan Moment. In the TRUE HORROR
section, I told a small portion of that dream of
what I had witness through the window of that
small cottage. And would you believe it, like

most things in this world. (STOLLEN). (2) Months later, what shall I see, before my very eyes? None other than an article in a local publication, entitled, YEP, The Michigan Moment. Now they never included Daddy's Horror. But no doubt it lay thought upon. I immediately saw fit to contact the paper and it's Editors. Warning them of consequences beyond my control if (sed), YES SED,,,,By now I assume you to be well acquainted with my style of laziness, my words of meaning. SED story is leaked. Less than a fortnight, I received an apology in the post. (JUST)

Never delve into family History. Unless of course, you bond that very Family. By Blood.

I have approach a many literary Agent. One being, DARLEY ANDERSON LITERARY, UK. Who I have yet to hear back from. Assuming they have received my submission. Never-the–less. I have been, on one occasion, approached by a man, stating that, his client, having looked over my shoulder, showed great interest in the purchase of my story. (€5,000,000.00) cash, he said. The whole story. We get the story, you live out the rest of your torrid life in luxury. "But it is not finished", I said. "AS IS", he stated. Take it or leave it, as he walked off. The next day I received an email stating the same, only this time in threatening tone. Because you can always tell the tone of a text or email right?. No. See, that's one of mine as well. "Downtown, Berlin, my reply. To the right you shall see The Ka DeWe. Head over left shoulder, a south facing street. Right in the middle is where I always stand. " Re: How shall I know you"? One may never possess the look of no one you have ever seen, nor shall you ever see once I have gone. As I emerge from shops, a 2016 Volvo limousine. Black, about 1/2 yards to my left. The back, passenger side door opens. An outstretch hand holding a very large briefcase are all I see. I never mount strange cars with strange men with strange penises, circumcised or No. Apart from which, I would never accept less than (€55,000,000.00) for a story such as mine. Never take me for the same fool you'd take others. Given my background, coupled with the current state of the economy, coupled with constant rising food cost, how in heaven's name, do you expect me to live out (100) years in luxury with a mere (5) million. In cash no doubt. What an insult. I have an (18) year old son, he has (18) best friends in the same age range, that's (20) million in groceries. (10), for steak and eggs alone over a fort night. What am I to do, never feed them. Nor have you, the consideration of my Daughter and Grandchild. Heaven's sake. " Those figures were far from accurate", (20) million,?,,, on stakes,?,,, over a fortnight ? The time stated Mid Bloody Morning and I had yet to Lunch. The Capital amount raised little worry. Actually that briefcase looked as though they had been eating pizza. Something had splatted on it, even dried. I just had to get outta there.

SOME HISTORY

My (4) years in Berlin, the greater part of my time spent in KaDeWe. My shopping, people watching, I purchased my meats, breads, all of my clothes, my cosmetics.

MY food is always prepared to my like.

Blushing. I shall have my meat Blushing. Never medium rare. Never well done. Blushing. The meat she is done, but she is in love, so there is a hint of pink. If you are going to eat meat, you may as well enjoy it. It is of the utmost importance to Indulge in what you Desire, while you may afford it. And while you are bursting to know what KaDeWe is. It's very location. (KaDeWe): Kaufhaus des Westens

The Kaufhaus des Westens, usually abbreviated to KaDeWe, is a Thai-owned department store in Berlin. With over (60,000) square meters of selling space and more than (380,000) articles available, it is the largest department store in Continental Europe.

MORE CRAP 2 READ

Everything should be everything. If you are going to live this ridiculous life, make the best of it. Do, what you do, with Great Detail while there is still time. This World is in for a rude bit of change. As one of the biggest fans of Supply and Demand, I am saddened to say. Old Devils, they are the pair of them. Stumbling fingers locked toward a cliff over jagged rock. If you fancy something, STOK-UP, as someone advised me Decades prior. I am no brag. I only mean to say, that if you are going to do something, do it. Do it well. You have to dress anyway, or go outside naked. So why never dress up. No longer do I wish to see women, out with their husbands, in a state of dress which suggest, she has been gardening. Hot rollers were invented for a reason, as were the Frock and the High Heeled Shoe.

___GOODS TO STORE: ___

PAPER TOWEL ROLLS

HAIR PRODUCTS

YOUR FAVOURITE COSMETICS

NOODLE PACKS

WATER

UN-REFRIGERATED JUICES

CANNED GOODS

RICE, SPECHETTI, BEANS

BREAD (FREEZE IT)

VEGATABLES (SLICE, CHOP, PLACE IN PLASTIC BAGS AND FREEZE THEM)

SODA (IF YOU CONSUME IT)

WOOL BLANKETS (KEEP IN COOL DRY SPACE)

PLASTIC BAGS

LARGE PIECES OF PLASTIC (OR TARPS) to cover windows

STRONG TAPE

A GENERATOR

BATTERIES

FLASHLIGHTS

LIGHTERS (Dangerous)

MATCHES (Dangerous)

KAROSINE, while it is still available. (BE CAREFUL, STORE OUTSIDE) dangerous. Store just enough to fill the heater in a single use

A KAROSINE HEATER (Dangerous)

VICES (whatever your addiction, cigars, cigarettes, etc. ..STOK -UP NOW) try to quit

BATH TOWELS

T-P (Bad Habit, Baby wipe shall suffice)

MORE WATER

DIAMONDS (to exchange for food)

CASH (While it is still worth something)

WARM CLOTHING

Leggings

Wool socks

Cashmere socks

Wool gloves

Leg warmers

Jumpers

Opaque tights

Stockings

Denims

Over-alls

Footed PJ's (Even the Adult ones)

HOT WATER BOTTLES

EMPTY WATER BOTTLES (to be used as hot water bottles)

WOOD (for fire)

WOODEN STRIKE ON BOX MATCHES (caution)

SOAP (No time for Mineral soaks, Salt rubs and Seaweed wraps).

TOOTH PASTE

BLEACH (store in a cool dry place)

91% ALCOHOL

VASALINE

VITAMIN E OIL

INDIVIDUALY WRAPED SNACKS AND GOODIES

VITAMINS (THE ONES YOU TAKE, THE ONES YOUR NEIGHBORS TAKE ETC.)

GARLIC (FRESH) while it may Destroy Certain Species of Vampire, It may well kill off certain species of CANCER.

GARLIC (ODERLESS SOFTGELS) Take 2 Daily, Starting NOW. (nO mORE RX)

FRUIT (CHOP AND FREEZE)

CANNED MILK

A GLUE GUN

GLUE STIX

COOKING OIL

DISH LIQUID

DISH SCRUBBY PADS (FOIL)

ALL-CLAD- POTS, PANS, WOKS, DOUBLE BOILERS, ETC

ASPERIN (ANADIN)

NYQUIL

OTC TYLENOL

NUROFEN

VAPOR RUB

LEATHER JUMP (combat) BOOTS

THERMALS

WOOL SCARVES

CAMPING TENTS

ELECTRIC EXTENSION CORDS

THICK STRONG ROPE

ADAPTERS

LIGHT BULBS

PET FOOD etc. (litter)

LOVED ONES (Forgive Them, Hug, Repeat)

HEADE

THE WORLD SHALL SOON GROW COLD
AND DARK. THERE WILL BE NO MORE
SHOPS BECAUSE THERE SHALL BE NO
MORE SUPPLIERS. NO MORE STOCK
MARKET. NO MORE GROWERS. NO MORE
SHALL THERE BE A NEED FOR MONEY,
ONCE MAN OPENS HIS EYES. SO UNTIL
WE FAMILIARIZE OUR SELVES WITH THE
WAY THINGS SHOULD HAVE BEEN, WE
SHALL SPEND GENERATIONS IN A GREAT
MISS OF WHAT WE USE TO HAVE, NEED.
THINGS OF WHICH WE HAVE GROWN
ACCUSTOM. WHAT WE CANNOT DO
WITHOUT, OR SO WE HAVE BEEN LEAD
TO BELIEVE THERE WILL BE NO MORE SKY
MILES, NO ONE TO IMPRESS.

As you ponder my message, and you have stocked your pantry, relax. Watch some tele. Why not enjoy the time we have left as we go about our lives in a dark haze of smoke which reads, in large white chalk drawn letters. (I am always Going to Be OK, I am always going to be able to Globe trot or run to the shops for what I need).

IF YOU LOVE, NEED SOMETHING, STOK-UP, OR JUST WAIT TIL WE ALL DISAPEAR, THEN SIMPLY PICK IT UP FROM THE FLOOR. .

NOW: As we sit on our Jaxes awaiting World Destruction. Foods to make tele viewing better: (Cookbook for The Lonely Hearted)

1. Peter Kay Car Share: Chilly Cheese Chips, (Fries), Chicken Wing Dings (Doused in Frank's Red Hot Sauce). Barbequed Chicken's Wing with a good mash and Peas drowned in a full- bodied beef gravy.

2. Pink Panther Cartoon: Hot Cocoa, Kosher Hot Dogs. A freshly baked bun and no toppings.

3. Are you being Served: Hot Tea, Sandwich, Soup, Peas and Mash, Bangers. Or Egg and Chips.

4. (MST3K) Mystery Science Theatre 3000: Home Made Spaghetti, Garlic Bread, Red Wine. Vegetable Soup with Fried bread.

5. Keeping Up Appearances: Hot Tea with Biscuits, or a well iced cake.

6. Goose Bumps: Oreo Cookies, Milk. Pizza, Crisps, Chocolate Bar.

7. Scream 1 (NO NEED FOR SEQUALS): Hot

Buttery Popcorn, Slushy.

8. Classic Horror Films (aka) Hammer Films. (UK): Hot Lamb Chili, Fruit Smoothie, Pita with Hummus, Follow with a Big Slice of Chocolate Cake, Hot Coffee, or Cabernet.

9. SNL: Soda, Crisps, Let overs, cold thai, Heated Thai, Take Away, or popcorn, Chocolate.

10. BBC World News: Hot Coffee with Cream, or Pour a Good Hot Jamaican blue Mountain over Vanilla Hagan Daaz.

11. Bloomberg: Hot Coffee, Toast, (1) Egg Over easy, Turkey Sausage. Or Hot Coffee, Waffles with hot Maple Syrup.

12. Surfing the Web: PIZZA, Grape Soda, Chocolatey sweets.

13. Loose Women: Wine or Hot Tea, box of Godiva Chocolates. Chocolate covered strawberries.

14. Lorain: Cole Slaw, Corned Beef, Sliced Tomatoes, Green Peas.

15. East Enders: NEVER WATCH.....They Killed off Fat Boy, Remember.

16. Coronation Street: Thai.

17. Peppa Pig: Spaghetti, or Canned Spaghetti Rings.

18. Harold and Kumar go to White Castle: DUH!!!!!!! or Shake Shack.

19. Scooby Doo Cartoons: Cheetos, Nearly frozen Soda, Chocolatey sweets. Hot Cocoa, with Cayenne pepper. A well-dressed Chicago Dog (ADD KATSUP)

20. Lupin the III Cartoon: Southeast Australian Red, Or a Good Scotch. Day old reheated Thai. Hot, Spicy Shrimp with White rice. Godiva Truffles (pasticcio).

21. Cowboy Bebop Cartoon: Champagne, or Moet Black Label with Cold Pizza, or Cold Chicken and Wedding Cake (If Available). Perhaps, a nice room temperature Paradise.

22. Shin Chan Cartoon: RAMEN NOODLES and Beer. A well done crispy pan fried salmon cake.

23. Agatha Kristie's, Marple. The ones starring Geraldine McEwan: Fish and Chips, Biscuits, Hot Mint Tea. Sliced Tomato, Cole Slaw. Sherry

24. France 24 (French Version): Hot Coffee, two sugars, one cream.

25. Jonny Test; (Cartoon): Strawberry Fizzy drinks, If you dare. Cheese crisps and your favourite chocolates.

26. The Catherine Tate Show: Whatever you have in the pantry, but you had better eat something.

27. 1941 Topper Returns: Chocolate Cake, Tea or Coffee. Spaghetti, Chicken. Beans Soup with a Good Crusted Bread. Lobster, Champagne. A well designed Vinaigrette coated Salad, Deliciously Pleasing to the eye.

28. Diners Drive-ins and Dives (Triple D): Whatever they are eating. Trust me you had better stand at preparedness.

29. AGETHA CHRISTIES: By The Pricking Of My Thumbs. Staring Geraldine MC -Ewin. IN MY OPINION THE (G.M). Episodes are King:
A good, strong, Mint Tea and Lemon Biscuits for the first half. After meeting Sweet Brother Noomsy, you may wish to go Ala-Carte on Fish n Chips with a good Crusted Bread, A rich Red Spicy to Hot Cocktail Sauce, chased by Best Quality Cognac (Hennessey).

30. AGETHA CHRISTIES: A Murder Is
Announced. (G.M) Episode, AGAIN:
A Plate of Red Vine Ripened Tomatoes, Douse
lightly with Apple Cider Vinegar, Salt and Cracked
Black Pepper. Delicious Butter Pound Cake. A
Freshly Brewed Kettle of Tea. Full English
Breakfast. Vegetable Stir Fry. Freshly Squeezed
Orange Juice. A really good Scotch.

31. Last of the Summer Wine: Iced Buns, Tea.
Salmon salad spread on a good crusted bread,
lettuce and tomato. Sheppard's Pie. Fish and Chips
with an ice cold Ale.

Would you were, hip on what to consume,
while the eye is capturing certain images, the
stomach may find itself best pleased. A relation
to knowing which colours fit your life. Simile:
I, myself, would never drive an Orange Car", I
once said. Is that never silly, someone asked.
NO. I would never drive a car in Blue green
either. The blue green would cause me to itch,
resulting in a bad days driving. No one needs
that. The Orange car would bring about bad
memories, same. I would never wear any
garment in the colour periwinkle, denotes
memories of my childhood. And we all know I
never need that in public society. When we
find what works with our chemistry, we live

more peaceful lives with fewer mishaps. An all-black car would boost my ego, maybe not good for the roads where normal people drive. An all Matte Black automobile and I are, YES ARE, spending more time outside of it in mad hope of attractive men observe me mounting the driver's seat. "Bum first", she said. As I swing my legs around. Still, never good. My mind should be on safe driving. A solid pepper white MINI anything, and I am so at ease that my day will go fine. I am more careful, because apart from denting it. I want, never a speck of dust to touch it.. Rather, it is a MINI. Choice Machines must be handled with the utmost Respect and Care. Everyone should find their equilibrium and stand parallel it. Find your equilibrium, stand as close as possible.

I COULD GO ON FOREVER. NO NEED TO CONSEVE PAPER. A TREE IS MORE THAN HAPPY TO GIVE HIS LIFE FOR THE CAUSE. A TREE HAS LIVED ITS LIFE TO PROVIDE. SAVE THE FORREST? NO WAY. WHY, WHAT FOR. A TREE UNDERSTANDS THE WAYS OF LIFE. OF NATURE. OF MAN. HE HOLDS IN EACH BRANCH, KNOWLEGDE, UNDERSTANDING AND A COMPLETE FAITH IN GOD. MORE VALUABLE THAN A DIAMOND. MORE VALUABLE THAN GOLD, (WOULD THEY WERE WORTH MUCH). MORE VALUABLE THAN MOST THINGS WE PLACE ON A HIGH SCALE AT (2) TO (3) MONTH'S SALARY. HE SITS FREE, IN REACH OF THE SKY AS HE CLEANS OUR AIR LOVING THE INSECTS, THE BIRDS AS HE PROVID-ETH HOMES FOR SUCH WITH LOVE AND RESPECT FOR ALL WHO (BENIETH) HIM.

OH, YEAH, AND I CHANGE MY MIND, I WANT THE PACEMAN.

I have agreed to go after the Book, before the kids so I'd best get going. The Willow Warbler has met up with Daddy and they have landed safely back home. As 4 me? I'm off to climb EVEREST. And as I reach its peak, I shall plant a pole, Raise a flag, Pitch a tent, Light a Bon fire. Then sit down and write you a Book explaining every step of the climb. I know, I know, but this time I promise never to mention a word about Mother. After all, I SHAUNT BRING HER along.

Thank You

Toinen

Story Line and Cover Illustration

by (9)

English Translation

By A.H.Sffitch

Negativity?

That were ALL Toinen

Rough Translation and Icebreaker

By Amnie Stoakley

(STOAKLEY): Last name: Stoakley

This is an English locational name of Anglo-Saxon origin. Recorded as Stockleigh, Stockley, Stoacley, Stoackley, Stoakley, Stockly and others, it originates from any of the places called Stockleigh or Stockley in the counties of Devonshire, Staffordshire and County Durham. The place names are first recorded respectively as Stochelie in the famous Domesday Book of 1086, Stochilea in the pipe rolls of 1170, and Stocaleia in the Subsidy Rolls of 1308. The meaning is either the wood from which stocks, that is to say tree stumps or logs were obtained, and derived from the Old English pre 7th Century word "stocc", meaning a stump, and "leah", a wood or glade. Alternatively it may describe a wood belonging to the farm, from the Old English "stoc", meaning a dairy-farm, and "leah" as before. John and Mary Stockley were early emigrants to the New World of the American colonies. They are recorded as obtaining tickets to sail to Jamaica on the ship the "Two Brothers" in February 1678. The first recorded spelling of the family name is shown to be that of Pagan de Stockleye. This was dated 1279, in the Hundred Rolls of Oxfordshire, during the reign of King Edward Ist of England and known as 'The Hammer of the Scots', 1272 - 1307. Surnames became necessary when governments introduced personal taxation. In England this was sometimes known as the Poll Tax. Throughout the centuries, surnames in every country have continued to "develop" often leading to astonishing variants of the original spelling.

THANKx

9 (THE NUMBER)

A. DICIANNOVEVENTIRE

ANHEUSER-BUSCH (For Refrigeration),,,,
Who fancies warm Root beer anyway?

ANTHROPOLOGIES

ALEX SAWYER

AMNIE STOAKLEY

ANDREW RAJDA

ANN DEMEULEMEESTER

ASANTE S. RAJDA

AUDI / PORSCHE

CADILLAC

CHARLIE CHAPLIN

CHRISTOPHER LEE

CLIVE SWIFT

DENNIS RAJDA

EDWARD FURLONG

FRANK THORNTON BALL

FREE PEOPLE (for dressing me) Can't write a
Best Seller wearing just any old thing.

GENERAL MOTORS

JACKIE COOGAN

JERRY LEWIS

JIM JONES

JOHN COOPER WORKS

JOHN INMAN

JOHN JACKSON

LENOVO

LOIS HILL

LOUXOI SHANE STOAKLEY

MICHAEL RAJDA

MICROSOFT

MIENNA S. RADJA

SIR. MILTON D. STOAKLEY SR.

NIKE

PETER SALLIS

MR. RAYONELLE STOAKLEY (UNCLE RAY)

RESTORATION HARDWARE

RICHARD VALENTE

RIVER PHOENIX

SCION AUTOMOTIVE AB

SHANE BERNARDO

STOCK DUDE

THE BROWN WELSHMAN

THE MILKMAN (not like THAT)

TREVOR COLLINS

AND YOU, THE READER

Do you recall those list that come out, such as the top (30) things that you must do before you die?

Congratulations, you have just completed number (31).

TO

MY

FAMILY

O grow up, it's merely a book. And Please
wear Black to my Funeral.

49,245 WORDS…. Minus this, SHE SAID.